North
of
Nowhere

North
of
Nowhere

LIZ KESSLER

CANDLEWICK PRESS

Copyright © 2012 by Liz Kessler

First published in Great Britain by Orion Children's Books, a division of the Orion Publishing Group

First U.S. paperback edition 2015

Library of Congress Catalog Card Number 2012954327
ISBN 978-0-7636-6727-6 (hardcover)
ISBN 978-0-7636-7672-8 (paperback)

18 19 20 21 22 23 BVG 10 9 8 7 6 5 4 3

Printed in Berryville, VA, U.S.A.

This book was typeset in Warnock Pro.

Candlewick Press
99 Dover Street
Somerville, Massachusetts 02144

visit us at www.candlewick.com

This book is dedicated to the RNLI,
whose amazing work saves the lives of
thousands of people out at sea every year.

Chapter One

I need to write it all down. That's the only way I'll believe it's true.

Spring break, eighth grade. All those incredible, impossible things. Did they really happen? I've tried a hundred times to tell myself that they couldn't have. That none of it is possible. And I'm right; none of it *is* possible.

But that doesn't change the fact that it is true. Everything *did* happen, exactly as I'm going to tell it now.

The day began like the first day of any other school holiday. Dad was in bed with a cup of coffee and the Saturday paper. Mom was on the phone to Gran. Jamie, my older brother, was at the music shop in town where he's had a weekend job for the last two years. I was in my room, getting ready to go out to meet my friends.

For about another three minutes, the biggest concerns in my life were which belt went best with my new top and whether or not to put my hair up.

Then Mom finished on the phone and called me down to the kitchen. And that was pretty much the moment my life changed forever.

Not that I knew it, yet.

The first indication that things weren't right was that Mom didn't even use my proper name. Or, rather, she *did* use my proper name. That was the problem.

Amelia.

No one had called me Amelia for ages. When I began middle school a couple of years ago, everyone started calling me Mia. Then last summer, before eighth grade, I decided "Amelia" was officially banned. Everyone had called me Mia ever since. Even Mom didn't use my old name anymore; she knew how much I hated it.

But she did today.

"Amelia, darling," she called from the kitchen. "Before you go out, I'd like to ruthlessly destroy your life by taking you to the middle of nowhere, where you'll die a slow death from boredom, loneliness, and a general lack of anything that makes life worth living."

OK, to be fair, those weren't her *precise* words. What she actually said was, "Amelia, pack a bag. We're going to your gran's."

Which amounted to the same thing.

I opened my bedroom door and called down the stairs, "I'm going out with my friends!"

"Don't shout down the stairs to me!" Mom yelled back, kind of forgetting that she was the one who'd started the whole shouting up and down the stairs thing.

Unfair!

It was on the tip of my tongue to shout back and say so, when I had a better idea. I'd recently developed a new tactic that I called the "Be Nice" approach. I'd used it a lot lately and had found it to be quite effective in emergency situations. And finding out that your spring break has been effectively canceled and replaced by a trip to the back of beyond would surely count as an emergency in anyone's book.

I took a breath, practiced my "Be Nice" face in the mirror, and went downstairs.

Mom was hunched over the kitchen table, her head in her hands. I ran straight over, forgetting to put on a pretend face or come out with a rehearsed line.

"Mom, what is it?" I asked.

She let out a breath. "I don't know what to do," she said. "It's . . ."

I waited for her to continue. Running a hand through her hair, she shook her head. "I'm sure it's nothing," she said, forcing a bright smile onto her face.

The only problem was, I knew that smile. It was the one she used whenever Dad decided to give her a "treat" and make dinner. It was the one she used that time I came home from town with a tiny new miniskirt that I'd bought with my pocket money. And the one she used when Jamie brought home his new girlfriend who had a pierced nose and a ring through her eyebrow.

In other words, the one that was a total lie. Where do you think I learned my "Be Nice" trick?

"Mom, what's happened?"

Mom stopped pretending to smile. "It's your grandad," she said.

Which changed things a bit. See, Grandad is one of my favorite people in the world. I wasn't crazy about going to visit him and Gran, but that wasn't their fault. It was just that they lived so far away, in Porthaven, a tiny town where there was absolutely *nothing* interesting to do, and where everyone was either a fisherman or a hundred years old or both.

Gran and Grandad had grown up there. Gran's parents used to run the local pub. Gran and Grandad had moved down to live near us when Jamie was a toddler and I was a baby, but when my great-grandparents both died a few years later, Gran and Grandad inherited the pub. They hemmed and hawed for ages, but finally decided to move back to Porthaven and run it themselves.

The town had three shops and one pub, which I was only allowed into because it was Gran and Grandad's. Other than that — nothing. No cell-phone signal. No public transportation. No satellite TV. There was barely *normal* TV; the reception was touch and go.

Up until last year, when I sat her down and explained it, Gran thought "broadband" was a wide piece of elastic. And she was typical of most of the people in the town. I once mentioned the World Wide Web to one of the fishermen down at the harbor. He gave me a funny look, then he laughed and opened his arms out wide toward the sea as if he could hold the expanse of the ocean in them. "That's my wide world out there," he said. Then he picked up his fishing net and added, "And that's the only web I need for it."

I gave up trying to explain the Internet to anyone else in Porthaven after that.

But Grandad was different. He understood me better than Gran did. It wasn't that she and I didn't get along; we'd just never found any common ground. My world was about being with my best friends, Jade and Ellen. It was about going to movies, hanging out at the mall, and checking out celebrities in all the trashy magazines. Gran's world was about running the local pub in a tiny town, chatting with a few old fishermen, and making beds in the guest rooms they ran above the pub.

I suppose that was Grandad's world too, but at least he always took an interest in mine. He'd ask me what the number one songs were, or if I'd watched anything funny on YouTube lately. It always made me laugh when he said it. Partly because he was quite old, and old people don't really watch YouTube. And partly because they didn't even have the Internet, so I knew he didn't really understand what I was talking about.

But at least he made the effort. That was the difference between them. He tried to bridge the gap.

Well, I didn't know it yet, but Gran and I would soon find out that our worlds weren't quite so far apart, after all. We were about to discover exactly how much we *really* had in common.

But I'm getting ahead of myself. We need to get back to the kitchen, because my mom's eyes had started to water.

"Mom, what's happened to Grandad?" I asked.

Mom turned to look at me. "He's left," she said.

"Left? What do you mean? Left what? Why?"

"I don't know," she said. "It seems he and your gran had a bit of an argument a couple of days ago, and he's gone."

"Gone? What do you mean, gone? Gone where?" I knew I wasn't asking very clever questions, and they probably weren't helping, but I couldn't think of anything else to say. Grandad—gone? She must have gotten it wrong.

"We don't *know* where he's gone; that's the problem," Mom said. "He left a note, but Gran says she can't make heads or tails of it. To be honest with you, I could hardly even tell what she was saying between the crying."

Crying?

OK, I haven't told you that much about my gran yet, but here's one thing that anyone who knows her will tell you: Gran does *not* cry. Ever.

I remember as a kid, watching the sappiest films in the world with her, sobbing my eyes out, and Gran would sit there looking like a wax model — no emotion. I used to wonder if she had feelings at all, or if she kept them buttoned up somewhere inside her, as though they were wrapped in a big coat that she never took off.

I turned back to Mom. "Gran was crying?" I asked, just to make sure I'd heard right.

Mom nodded.

Which was when I knew there was no point in arguing.

I squeezed Mom's hand, and then I went up to my bedroom to pack.

"Why didn't Jamie have to come?" I asked, ten minutes into the five-hour drive, as I fiddled with the radio to find a decent station.

"I've already told you," Mom said. "Jamie's sixteen,

you're thirteen. It's fine for him to be in the house while Dad's at work. And anyway, he's working all week at the record shop."

To be honest, I wasn't all that bothered about Jamie not coming along. We argued most of the time anyway, so it would have just made the week even more difficult than it was already going to be.

I finally found some decent music on the radio. I closed my eyes and tried not to think about how much I was going to miss Jade and Ellen and all the things we'd planned.

And, more than anything, I tried not to think about how worried I was about Grandad.

"Drop off your stuff and come downstairs. Lynne, you can go in Room Four; it's the one at the end. The first three bedrooms are taken. Amelia, you can have Room Five across the hall, as long as we don't get any last-minute bookings. If we do, you'll have to share with your mom. I'll put the teakettle on." Gran abandoned us on the landing and went back downstairs to the pub.

I dragged my bag down the hallway. "I'm not *Amelia*," I mumbled.

Mom touched my arm. "Please, darling, don't make a fuss. She's got enough on her plate. We don't need to add anything else. Can't you just put up with it for a week?"

She was right. Grandad had disappeared into thin air. The last thing Gran needed was me fussing over what she called me. "OK," I said glumly.

Mom smiled. "Thank you. Now, get yourself unpacked and I'll see you downstairs, OK?"

I pushed open the door to guest bedroom number five. It was about half the size of my bedroom at home. The bed took up most of the space, with just enough room to squeeze in a nightstand on either side, a wardrobe in one corner, a sink in another, and a window on the opposite wall.

I pulled back the curtain and looked out the window. It was drizzly and gray out, and little spots of moisture dotted the windowpane. I rubbed my arm over them, wiping a space so I could see the line of roofs and chimneys sloping down to the small harbor. Beyond the harbor was the sea, stretching on forever. There was a blurry line where the sea met the sky, but on a gloomy February day, it was hard to tell where one ended and the other began.

I stood in the window, watching the grim stillness. After a few minutes, someone appeared in front of a house and scurried, head down, along the harbor front.

Then nothing. No noises. Nothing moved. Nothing happened. The loudest sound was the window shutter creaking in the wind.

A whole week without talking to my friends?

For the fiftieth time, I checked the signal on my cell phone. Still nothing. The room suddenly felt a bit smaller, and the air a bit thinner.

Mom knocked softly as she popped her head around the door. "Amelia, are you coming down?"

"Mom, it's not Amel—" I began.

"We agreed," she said firmly. "It's just for a week. Come on."

I rubbed my sleeve over the breath marks I'd left on the window, and I left the claustrophobic room behind me.

Mom linked her arm with mine. "We'll be OK, sweetheart," she said. "Let's just make sure your gran is too, eh?"

I nodded. "Sorry, I don't mean to be selfish," I said. "It's just . . ."

"I understand," Mom said, patting my arm. "I know how much this week meant to you. I'm sorry I had to drag you away. But we're here now; let's make the most of it."

"OK," I agreed. "We're here for Gran."

"That's the spirit," she said. "I've just called Dad to let him know we've arrived safely. He sent you this." She planted a kiss on the top of my head, and smiled at me. "Come on, then," she said, and I followed her downstairs.

We went through the door to the bar at the back of the pub. I ducked under the counter and followed Mom through to the lounge, where we pulled up a couple of seats at one of the big wooden tables. Three men were sitting at the bar, talking and drinking pints. An older couple was sitting at a table, heads close together as they shared a bottle of wine. Gran came through from the kitchen with a pot of tea.

"Fetch the rest of the things, will you, Amelia, dear?" she said to me, pointing at a tray of teacups on the bar.

I bit my tongue and didn't say anything about my name. "Sure," I replied with a "Be Nice" smile. I caught Mom's eye and she gave me a grateful nod.

Gran poured three cups of tea and we sat in awkward silence. Mom tried to look Gran in the eye, I tried to think of something to say, and Gran tried to pretend nothing was wrong as she slowly added milk to the cups.

Finally, Gran sat back and put her hands in her lap.

"So," she said. "I suppose you're wondering what this is all about."

Um. Well, that is *why we've traveled all day to be here.*

"In your own time," Mom said softly.

"Well, I can't say I understand the half of it," Gran said, "but I'll start from the beginning, and I'll tell you what I can."

Mom picked up her cup of tea and took a sip. I noticed her hands were shaking. As she caught my eye, I realized I was just as nervous. What were we about to hear? What kind of a week was in store?

And what exactly *had* happened to Grandad?

Chapter Two

"It started last weekend," Gran began. "He woke up on Saturday morning and announced that we were going away. Said we needed a break, and he wanted to take me on a romantic vacation."

"Did he have somewhere in mind?" Mom asked.

"He said I could choose. Anywhere I wanted."

"So what was the problem?" I asked.

"The problem was that it had to be this week, when we had three rooms already booked out. For the first time in Porthaven's history, the town council has gotten it together to run a few events for tourists, and we'll probably have our biggest takings in the pub since last season. Grandad expected me to cancel everything and run off on a silly whim with him." She paused and took a breath. "Plus, we've had one disastrous vacation this year already," she added tightly.

"What trip was that?" I asked.

Gran sighed. "That was a silly whim of his, too. It was just before Christmas. Oh, I remember now — it was the day the new brochures had come out."

"What new brochures?"

"The brochures advertising Porthaven's scheme to become some kind of wonderful vacation destination — as if!" she snorted. "Harry from the town council came around to ask if we'd help distribute them. Your grandad snatched a brochure and practically shoved Harry out of the house. Next thing I knew, he'd disappeared upstairs — then he came down half an hour later telling me he was taking me away for the weekend."

"So what was the disaster?" Mom asked.

"Well, we went away and it was all very lovely — for the first night. Then Grandad went out for a walk the next morning and came back with a migraine like I'd never seen before. He spent the entire day lying in our room in the dark. I was quite worried about him, but thankfully it passed. Some vacation, though!"

"So he was trying to take you away for a better weekend?" I asked.

"Seems like it."

"But you said no," Mom put in.

"Of course I did," Gran said sharply. To be fair, she does say a lot of things sharply, so it wasn't that unusual. Then she frowned. Also not unusual. Then she said, "Do you know the strange thing?"

Mom and I both shook our heads.

"I don't think he meant it," Gran said quietly.

"Why not?" I asked.

"He must have known I wouldn't just shut up shop and run away from home. He can't seriously have thought for a moment that I'd say yes."

"What are you suggesting?" Mom asked.

Gran sighed. "I don't know. I don't know *what* I'm suggesting. But he knows what I'm like. It's all very well for him to have these silly ideas. He's the one who sits drinking with the regulars, telling jokes, and sharing stories and laughs. I'm the one who keeps the books, and plans ahead, and makes sure that we stay afloat. He *knows* that. He must have known I wouldn't do something so childish and irresponsible."

She was right. Gran ran their lives like a sergeant major. "So why did he ask you if he knew you'd say no?"

"I don't know," Gran said. "I can't help wondering if he's just fed up. We've talked about retiring lately — but I can't see how we could do it. Maybe this is his solution: run away from it all."

Then she paused. There was something else troubling her. I could see it in her eyes — not that she'd ever admit it. Gran sees admitting to problems as a sign of weakness. "Of course, there is one other possibility," she said.

"What's that?" I asked.

"That he wanted an excuse to get away from *me*. Pretending he wanted us to take a vacation that he knew I would never agree to. Then when I said no, I was the baddie and he could go off with a clear conscience, telling himself he gave me every opportunity to go with him."

Mom reached across the table to take Gran's hand. "He wouldn't do that. He wouldn't just leave you like that."

Gran looked at Mom's hand on hers for a second, then she slipped her hand away and smiled a brittle smile at us both. "I know, dear. I'm sure he wouldn't. There'll be an explanation for the fact that I woke up yesterday morning in a cold bed, with my husband nowhere to be seen. I'm sure there will."

When she put it like that, I had to admit it didn't sound too good.

Just then, one of the men at the bar leaned forward and shook the bell on the counter. "Service, please!" he called, smiling across at us as he waved his empty pint glass above his head.

Gran stood up. "Right. I've got a pub to run. Lynne, let me show you the ropes while we're relatively quiet. Then if we get busy later, you can look after the bar while I sort out everything else. Amelia, why don't you take the dog out? He's in the back. I've not had a chance to give him a proper walk yet today, what with . . . well, you know. It's not easy running the whole place on your own."

Mom followed Gran to the bar. I was only too happy to walk the dog, so I went through to the living room, where Flake, their five-year-old border collie, was lying on a rug in front of a gas fire. As soon as he saw me, he started wagging his shaggy tail, flapping it happily on the rug.

I knelt down and stroked his tummy. "Hey there, Flake," I said into his ears as I gave him a big cuddle. "You're the first happy face I've seen since I got here."

He jumped up and followed me out of the room. I

poked my head around the door to the pub. "I'll take him down to the beach," I called.

Mom looked across and smiled. "Thank you."

"Don't let him eat any dead crabs," Gran added. "They make him sick."

"I won't."

I ran upstairs to get my coat. When I came back down, Flake was waiting for me by the back door, wagging his tail furiously.

"Come on, boy, let's get out of here," I said, grabbing his leash from the back door and clipping it on to his collar. I buttoned up my coat and we scuttled down the road toward the beach and the harbor.

As I walked down the street, Flake trotting happily beside me, I couldn't help thinking again about the day I was supposed to have had today. I'd have been at the movie theater by now, eating popcorn and sharing gummy bears with Jade and Ellen. Instead, I was walking along an empty, narrow cobblestone road down to a harbor with five fishing boats and a bunch of seaweed for company.

I checked my phone as I reached the harbor. Still no signal. I shoved it back in my pocket and walked around the edge of the beach to the slipway.

Flake ran happily down onto the sand, yapping delightedly. I couldn't help thinking how nice it must feel to be a dog. They're always so happy, so easy to please. I'd always wanted one, but Mom and Dad had said no. They said it wasn't fair to have a dog when we're all out at work or school all day, so I've had to make do with two gerbils and a guinea pig. All of which I adore — but it's not the same. You can't take them for walks, and they don't wag their tails with delight every time you come into the room.

I used to have pictures of kittens and puppies and rabbits all over my bedroom walls. I took them down last year when I had a sleepover at my house with my new friends. I decided it was time to leave fluffy bunnies behind. Since then, it had been mostly boy bands and actors on my walls, but in my secret heart of hearts, I still missed the bunnies.

I picked up a stick, and in a flash, Flake was sitting in front of me, his tail thumping on the sand, his eyes focused on the stick. I threw it, and he raced off down the beach. A second later, Flake and stick were back at my feet. We played as we wandered along the beach, throwing and fetching sticks and bits of driftwood. For a moment, I almost forgot how miserable I was supposed to be. I couldn't help being influenced by Flake's perpetual happiness.

We reached the end of the beach. Now what? I didn't want to turn back. I couldn't face sitting in the pub for the rest of the day, listening to the old fishermen talking about their catches, or seeing Gran's pained face, or watching Mom's attempts at being a barmaid, while we all tried not to show how worried we were.

So, instead, I threw a few more sticks for Flake. At the end of the beach, there were three arches that led to a tiny spit of sand and an old concrete wall that was once a jetty. It hadn't been used for years. At high tide, it was cut off completely as the arches filled up with water.

I did a bad throw and the stick got carried along by the wind and went flying into the last archway. The tide was out, so Flake darted into the arch after the stick, and I waited for him to return, stick in mouth, tail wagging furiously. But he didn't.

A whole minute passed.

"Flake?" I walked down to the arch and poked my head around the edge of it. He wasn't in there. "Flake?" I called again, louder. No reply. No Flake.

I ducked down and walked through the arch to

the other side. It was more exposed on this side, and I turned my collar up against the cold. The wind was blowing sand across the surface of the beach, and carving tiny ripples across the tops of the waves farther out. I finally saw Flake, right at the end of the old jetty. He must have been chasing after the stick and lost track of where it had gone.

"Flake!" I shouted. He looked up briefly, but didn't come back. Instead, he just stood there, yapping away. Maybe there was a seal in the water or something. I looked around for a stick to distract him, but there was nothing on this side of the arches. Just the sand, smoothed flat by the retreating tide.

I ducked down, ran back through the arch, and found a stick. When I got back, Flake was still at the end of the jetty, jumping around excitedly, barking and wagging. I called him again. He ignored me again.

"Flake, what is it?" As I got closer, I could see what he was barking at: an old-fashioned fishing boat, like the ones in the harbor. It was tied up to the one hitching ring that remained on the very end of the old jetty, drifting around on its rope and bouncing on the water. I hadn't noticed it before. It must have been on the other side of the jetty, and the wind had blown it around while I was fetching the stick.

Flake wagged and yapped even harder as I approached. It was only once I got alongside the boat that I could see why he was so excited: there were three crab pots on board. He must have smelled them as soon as he came through the archway.

"Flake, you're not allowed to eat crabs — they make you sick."

As if he understood, Flake gave me a sorrowful glance and a miniscule whimper — and then, before I even realized what he was doing, he leaped across to the boat!

"Flake! What are you doing? It's not our boat!" I waved the stick in the air. "Look. Stick. Fetch!"

But Flake was too distracted by the crab pots to care about a boring old stick. He scratched at the sides of the pots, trying to lick them. Luckily, they were all empty. I wouldn't have wanted to have to tell Gran that Flake had eaten someone's entire day's crab catch. And I wouldn't have wanted to deal with the aftereffects either. I'd seen Flake when he'd been sick from eating something he shouldn't have, and without going into details, it wasn't pretty! Plus, I couldn't bear the sad, sorrowful look on his face when he didn't feel well.

"Flake, come on. Off the boat!" I called. He ignored me.

I stepped closer to the boat. It was right alongside the jetty now. Ropes lay on the deck in neat circles. A pile of fishing nets lay folded at the back. It had a tiny cabin in the middle with a big wooden wheel inside. The door was closed, with the crab pots leaning against it. Flake stood whining and scratching all around them.

"Flake, don't make me come on there and get you, or I'll be angry," I said as sternly as I could.

Flake *still* ignored me.

That was it. I *was* going to have to climb on board and fetch him.

I stepped across from the jetty and onto the side of the boat. Then I hopped down on the deck beside Flake. He jumped and looked at me with a startled expression.

"What? *You* can leap onto some random boat tied up out here in the middle of nowhere, but I can't?"

Flake wagged his tail.

"Is that your answer to everything?" I asked with a laugh. "Come on. We should get back."

I clipped his leash back on to his collar and turned to go. But as I swung around, the wind caught the side of the boat and we bobbed to the side so suddenly that I slipped against the rail. As I reached out to steady myself, I noticed a locker at the back of the boat. The catch was loose and the boat's motion had made the door swing right open.

I reached across to push it shut — but something inside the locker caught my eye. The late sun had slipped low enough to hit something shiny inside the locker. What was it?

I should probably have left it, but the reflection of the light was flashing right into my eyes. It felt almost as though it were spelling out a code, just for me, drawing me in — and I couldn't resist. Whatever was inside the locker flashed again. What was *in* there? I had to know!

I checked behind me to make sure no one was watching. I didn't really want to be seen reaching into someone's locker on a boat I shouldn't have even been on in the first place.

There was no one around.

Without pausing for another second, I knelt down, opened the locker, and reached inside.

Frank

He'd walked past the shop every day for two weeks. Each time, he felt his heart rate speed up. She was still there, standing in the courtyard. She was a beauty.

A twenty-foot skiff. Yellow hull, inboard diesel engine, mizzen sail at the back, wheelhouse just big enough for two in the center. She was exactly what he needed. Now that his wife had a child on the way, it was time to trade in his glorified rowboat. He could never catch enough fish to provide for a family in that.

He'd been to the bank this morning, and he finally got the loan he needed. He pulled out the letter from his pocket and read it for the twentieth time, just to be sure.

Yes, it was real. He had the money.

He pushed open the door. He'd never been inside before, and he hesitated in the doorway, looking around the busy shop. Shelves were crammed into every corner, each one stacked high with all manner of objects. There were ropes in a hundred lengths and colors, anchors in fifty sizes, cans of marine paint, oilskin coats, tubs and buckets — and, in between them, the most bizarre objects. A kitchen sink lay on its side in one corner, a large umbrella was propped over a garden gnome in another. A shelf full of animal ornaments; another of old books — it was as though the owner had emptied out a street of houses and crammed the contents into his shop.

Frank cleared his throat. "Hello?" he called.

He heard a rustling sound coming from a room at the back of the shop. A moment later, a young man appeared. He couldn't have been much more than a teenager — he was certainly younger than Frank. But in contrast to Frank in his Sunday best from visiting the bank, this young fellow looked as if he had just gotten out of bed.

His hair was wild and wavy — brown with light-blond streaks running through it. His face was pocked with what looked like acne scars, and his clothes were as odd and mismatched as his shop. Pale, baggy

27

trousers and a maroon shirt, half untucked and buttoned up wrongly. His eyes, piercing and green, found Frank's.

"I — I'm sorry to disturb you," Frank stammered.

The young man shrugged as he reached under his counter and brought up a pouch of tobacco and some papers. Rolling himself a cigarette, he offered the pouch to Frank.

"No, thanks," Frank said.

The man pulled a lighter from his pocket and lit his cigarette. Then he turned back to Frank. Pinching his cigarette between his teeth, he ran a nicotine-stained hand through his messy hair. "Eric Travers at your service," he said, as if pretending to be a grown-up. "How can I help you?"

Frank pointed outside. "The skiff," he said.

"Oh, yes, I've seen you looking at her. Have you made your mind up yet?" Eric asked.

"I made my mind up the first day I saw her," Frank replied. "I just had to persuade the bank manager to agree with me."

Eric laughed. "And has he?"

Frank took the letter from his pocket and handed it over.

Eric sat down on an old stool and scanned the letter. "Well, I'll just need a check and it looks like she'll be yours, then," he said.

Frank thrust his hands in his pockets to stop himself from jumping up and punching the air. "Really? Just like that?" He took his checkbook out, swiftly wrote a check, and handed it to Eric.

"Just like that," Eric said, scanning the check as he drew on his cigarette. Then he coughed, got up from his stool, and returned to the room at the back of the shop.

He was gone for almost five whole minutes. Was Frank supposed to wait here? Follow Eric into the back of the shop? Leave? What? He fidgeted from foot to foot, biting his nails and wondering what to do.

He was on the verge of turning to leave when Eric reappeared with a large bag in his hand. "Let's go and check her over," he said, and Frank followed him outside.

They looked over the boat together, Eric pointing out the controls, the hidden storage spaces, and so on, Frank taking it all in with wide eyes and a bursting heart. "You seem to know her inside out," he said.

"She was my pa's," Eric replied. "He packed her up years ago after a stormy trip and never went out on her *again. Said he'd gone off the sea, and he gave up the fishing life and opened Shipshape." Eric spread his arms wide to show what he had inherited. "Passed away five years ago."*

"I'm sorry," Frank said.

Eric nodded. "Been doing some cleaning of the place and I came across her again in the boat shed out back. Almost forgotten her, so I decided to dust her down and see if I could find her a good home."

"She'll have a good home with me," Frank said. "I promise."

"Aye, I reckon she will."

As they shook hands on the deal, Eric passed Frank the bag he'd been holding. "This goes with her." He pointed to the wheelhouse. "There's a holder in there. Fits like a glove."

Frank opened the bag. Inside was a brass compass, with a bouncing dial inside a glass dome. Frank looked up at Eric. "It's beautiful," he said.

"It's yours if you want it."

"How could I not want it?"

"Pa said it wasn't always . . . how shall I put it?" Eric looked to the sky. "Reliable," he said eventually. He dropped his cigarette on the ground and squished it with his foot.

"In what way?"

"Seems it behaves a bit odd at times," Eric said. "Pa wouldn't talk about it much — but between you and me, I always wondered if it had anything to do with him giving up the fishing. He said one thing that stuck in my head, though."

"What did he say?"

"He said most of the time it'd work like a dream. It could guide you to the other end of the world. But just now and then, if the compass was pointing north and a gust of wind hit from the opposite side, it would send the arrow spinning."

"A mechanical fault?" Frank asked.

"Call it what you like. Pa never had an explanation. Just said you could be sailing along quite happy till it happened. Then when it finished spinning, the arrow would still be pointing north, but you'd be somewhere else."

"Somewhere else? Like where?"

Eric shrugged. "'North of nowhere' was all he'd say."

Frank swallowed as a shiver went through him.

"Still want it?" Eric asked.

The man was just telling stories. He'd met the type before. Most of the fishing folk around here had a strange tale to tell about their travels on the sea. It wasn't going to put him off. "Yes, I still want it," Frank said. He took the compass from the shopkeeper.

Frank looked lovingly at his new boat, then turned to say thank you once more. Eric was at the door of his shop. "Thank you!" Frank called.

In reply, Eric waved a hand without turning around. "Look after her, and she'll look after you," he replied.

And then he was gone, and Frank was standing in the courtyard, holding the keys and the compass. He climbed aboard and looked proudly around at his new purchase. He took out the compass and opened the door to the wheelhouse.

As he slotted it carefully into place, he shook himself and banished the shopkeeper's silly stories from his mind.

Nothing was going to ruin this day. The day he had finally become a proper fisherman — and soon to be a father, too. He kissed the anchor pendant he always wore around his neck and thanked his lucky stars.

North of nowhere, indeed. This boat was going to take him everywhere!

Chapter Three

Flake was suddenly more interested in what I was doing than in the crab pots. Maybe he'd finally realized there were no crabs inside, so there was no point in trying to get into them.

Or maybe he was as intrigued as I was.

I felt around inside the locker and pulled out the only thing in there. It was a book, only it wasn't like any book I'd ever seen. Its cover was dark-brown leather, with paler leather strips woven into patterns, around and around in a spiral.

In the center of the spiral was the thing that had caught the sunlight: a shiny golden stone. It was beautiful. The whole book was. It felt like something from an ancient magician's study.

I lifted the book and sniffed it. Strong, old leather. I glanced around again, feeling like a thief, and then I opened the book. Even the pages were unusual: thin, wispy paper with tiny watermarks on every page.

I'd never really written a diary, but if I'd had a book like this I bet I would have. With a book like this, you could write anything. The pages were filled with tiny, neat handwriting.

I knew I shouldn't, but I couldn't stop myself. I flicked to a random page.

I'm so bored. The weather was bad today, so no school again. It's not that I love school. It's just something to do. And it means seeing my friends. I wish the other girls didn't all live on the mainland. I hate being different from everyone else — and having to depend on the weather and the tides in order to get to school on time.

I wouldn't mind missing school so much if I were allowed to sleep in and do nothing, or perhaps spend all day in front of the fire reading a book. That would be SO nice!

But, no. As soon as Father told me I wasn't going to school, that was it. Mother had me up cooking, fixing, painting, generally helping with all the most boring chores in the world. Honestly, sometimes I feel like a servant!

I'm sorry. I know that's unfair. And I wouldn't say it out loud to anyone. This is the only place in the world that I can confess how I really feel. Dear diary, where would I be without you? You're like my best friend. The best friend that I haven't got, because who wants a best friend that you have to travel out on a choppy ocean to visit — assuming you have access to a boat in the first place?

It's not fair. I'm thinking of going on strike. Or running away.

Exactly. Thinking of. That's all I ever do. Think. Dream. Imagine a different life.

Oh, well. Mother's calling. Better go.

See you later,

D

I stared at the page—and suddenly I felt worse than a thief. I shouldn't read more—I knew I shouldn't pry—but this "D" person sounded just like me! I felt as if I understood her completely. She was the first person I'd ever come across in Porthaven who seemed to speak my language. And the first one who sounded as fed up as I was. Maybe she'd *want* to share her thoughts with me.

I turned to the next page.

Dear Diary,

First of all, I must apologize for yesterday. I was in such a foul mood. I feel sorry for you sometimes. You get all of my tempers and grumps. I hope you forgive me!

As it happened, the day turned out wonderfully after all. When I went out to bring in the laundry, I noticed some activity down in the bay. I pulled the clothes down quickly as I could, and I called to Mother. She came to look, and we both agreed it was probably the seals — but neither of us could see what they were getting so excited about.

I left Mother with the laundry and ran down to the cove, to get a better look. And guess what! Seal pups! Right there in our bay. Oh, they were the sweetest things! A whole crowd of them, maybe twenty or more, with their mothers. All of them splashing around, popping their little heads up and then diving back down, while their mothers chased after them to feed and clean them.

I love my life so much. I never ever want to live anywhere but Luffsands!

Lots of love,

D

She loved animals as much as I did! She sounded even *more* like me! I thumbed through the diary and flicked open another random page.

It's raining and I'm stuck inside. I can't go out and look for interesting wildlife, or pick some early snowdrops. I'm bored. Lonely. Fed up. Sometimes I feel that there isn't a single person in the world who I can talk to, or who understands me. I have friends, of course. But we never really talk about anything that matters, and they don't _really_ understand my life. _They_ don't have to depend on the weather and the elements and their parents just to get back and forth.

It's not fair. I said as much to Mother the other day, but she replied that I was a lucky girl and should be grateful for the life we have. Father just *laughed and shook his head. He wouldn't want another life even if it came with a million dollars!*

I wish I had a true friend here in our funny little village — and more things to do so I wouldn't get so bored. Maybe I should write more than just a diary. Perhaps I could pretend that this room is my secret turret in a castle and that these pages are my very own novel. Then I could hide from the world and write night and day, and I wouldn't mind so much. With this beautiful book, I feel I could write anything.

That was what I'd just thought—almost word for word! She was *exactly* like me! Only, she didn't have a best friend. That was really sad. Maybe *I* could be her best friend, at least for the week. I didn't have *any* friends here!

I turned to the final entry. It had today's date on it.

So here I am, sitting in the boat in Porthaven harbor, waiting for Father again. He always takes SO long. He told me to be back promptly, so I abandoned my friends and came to meet him. Now I'm thinking I could have had another half an hour with them, as I've been sitting on my own wait-

ing all that time. I'll give him a few more minutes and then I'm going to look for him. He said he'd be back right after the auction, but I know what he's like. He's probably in the pub with his friends.

The pub! D's dad was one of the men from Gran and Grandad's pub. Maybe we knew him. Maybe I'd even seen her!

I read on.

I'm looking forward to tomorrow. Father has promised I can help him at the auction. Not that that kind of thing usually excites me, but the auction at the Sunday market is always a bit different, and my friends will be there with their families too. With any luck, we can all give our parents the slip and have some fun while they do their boring business!

OK. He should definitely be here by now. I'm going to go and look for him.

See you later, diary,

D

I closed the diary and placed it back in the locker. Suddenly, I was torn between feeling guilty for reading someone else's private diary and being excited at the thought that I might actually have found someone in this town who I could be friends with.

"What do you think, Flake? Shall we try to find the mysterious 'D'? Hey, that's almost a name! I'm going to call her 'Dee' from now on!"

Flake looked up at me and wagged his tail. I laughed and reached down to give him a hug.

Whatever I decided to do, I had to go back to the pub first. It was starting to get dark. I must have been out for at least an hour, and Mom and Gran would be wondering where we were.

Flake and I jumped off the boat and walked back up to the beach. Flake chased seagulls and barked at seaweed while I hurried back toward town, wondering if my new friend might even be waiting for us in the pub.

"There you are! Get Flake in the back and dry him off, and then you can help us collect some glasses," Gran said as she offered me a grateful nod and a tight smile.

I decided that Gran's welcome was really her way of saying, "Oh, you darling girl, you've been gone ages. We really missed you, as we love your company more than anything and hate it when you're not here," and I went in the back to do as she said.

I dried Flake with an old towel that hung on the back door. I was more than happy to help collect glasses, as it gave me a chance to check out everyone in the pub and see if I could find Dee's dad — and maybe even Dee herself.

Only, there was no one within about fifty years of my age, and I was pretty sure that none of the men were Dee's dad, either. For one thing, they all looked too old, and for another — well, they just didn't look how I imagined her dad to look.

I spent the next half hour helping to clear tables and wash glasses, and trying not to think too much about how slowly time passed in Porthaven.

I was just starting to feel in desperate need of an escape when Gran gave me one.

"Amelia, dear, would you empty the trash, please?" she said. "Put it in the big green garbage can at the end of the path."

Normally, taking a bag of trash out would have been fairly near the bottom of any list of things I would be likely to get excited about, beaten only by chewing off my own toes and eating them for dinner. But on this occasion I didn't mind.

I pulled on my coat, grabbed the smelly trash bag, and took it outside to the green waste bin.

Then I glanced down the road toward the harbor.

Maybe the boat was still there. Perhaps I'd just missed Dee and her dad leaving the pub.

I could be there and back in less than ten minutes. Gran wouldn't even notice how long I'd been gone. And if she did, I could always say the bag split and I had to scrabble around picking up all the trash or something.

Before I could talk myself out of it, I was running back to the beach.

Dee wasn't there — and neither was the boat. I'd missed them. I'd have to wait till the next day. Grandad had told me about the Sunday market, but we'd never been here when it was on before.

I consoled myself with the thought that we could probably go along, and with the hope that, by this time tomorrow, Grandad might have turned up and I might have found a new friend.

Surely something good had to happen at *some* point this week — didn't it?

Chapter Four

For once, I was up and dressed before Mom called me. She knocked softly and poked her head around the door.

"Good grief," she said, looking at her watch. "Has my watch stopped? Or am I still asleep and dreaming?"

Yes, ha-ha, Mom. Very funny.

"It's a nice day and I thought I'd get up early and walk the dog," I replied.

Mom glanced at the window. Rain ran down the glass in long, wiggly streaks.

"OK, maybe it's not a nice day. But I thought I'd get up anyway. It's not a crime, is it?"

"I suppose, strictly speaking, it wouldn't be classified as an *actual* crime," she said. "But I'm fairly certain it would be listed under Highly Unusual Activity." Then she smiled and held out her hand. "Come on, Mia, love. Let's go and get some breakfast before you go out."

And because she called me Mia, I decided to forgive her sarcasm.

I scarfed down my breakfast as fast as politeness and the risk of indigestion would allow, and then I took my plate to the sink and grabbed Flake's leash from the back door. "Can I take Flake out now?" I asked.

"That would be lovely," Gran replied, with another of her tight smiles. Actually, this one was even tighter than the ones she'd managed to squeeze out so far. She still hadn't heard anything from Grandad.

It had been two days now.

I kept telling myself there must be a totally logical explanation for his disappearance. He couldn't have left her. He wouldn't have just gone like that. Not without explaining. He wouldn't leave her, and I *knew* he wouldn't leave me.

I didn't want to think about it. It made my stomach tighten up and growl painfully when I did, so instead I concentrated as hard as I could on putting Flake's leash on and grabbing a ball from his box of toys.

"See you soon," I called over my shoulder. I shut the door behind me and turned to Flake. "OK, boy, shall we go to the harbor and see if Dee's boat's there? We're going to make a new friend today!"

Flake flapped his tail excitedly on the ground. You'd really only have to look at Flake or throw a tiny piece of debris across a beach to make his day. Shame it wasn't so easy for humans.

I threw the ball a few times for Flake. Each time he brought it back to me, he'd drop the ball, then turn and snuggle into my legs for a cuddle.

"Flake, you are definitely the best thing about this place," I whispered into his fur as I squeezed him tightly and kissed his head. Then I put his leash on and crossed to the other side of the harbor, where the fish auction was held.

But when we arrived at the auction hall, the doors were closed. I tried to push them open, but there was a bar across them with a padlock dangling from it.

I walked all around the building, looking for another way in. There wasn't one.

Around the back, there was a man in a canvas jacket and rain boots, sitting on a wooden container untangling a knotted-up mass of green rope. He looked up as Flake and I appeared in front of him.

"All right there? Need some help?" he asked.

"I — um, I was looking for the auction," I said awkwardly. "I thought it was today."

"Auction's Monday, Wednesday, and Friday."

"But the one that's part of the Sunday market. Isn't that here, too?"

The man shook his head. "Not this week, my dear. Auctioneer's sick. It'll be back on next week."

I turned to leave. "Oh. Sorry. Thanks."

Flake and I tromped back around to the beach. Dee had probably heard that the market was off and hadn't bothered coming. So much for my new best friend. So much for the wonderful day I was going to have. All I'd managed to do was wake up so early that there was even more day to get through!

I moped along the beach while Flake picked up every bit of wood he could find and dropped each piece at my feet. I threw them for him, but my heart wasn't in it anymore. Soon, we were back at the arches. The tide was a bit higher than the last time I'd been down, and there were pools of water under the arch. I rolled up my pant legs over my boots and waded through to the other side. I wasn't even sure why I was bothering, as the boat obviously wasn't going to be there. But I couldn't resist having a look, just in case.

We came out on the other side of the arches and crossed the spit of sand to the jetty.

It was there! The boat was there! Dee *was* in Porthaven after all! But where was she? And if the market wasn't on, why had they come?

I looked around, searching for anything that might answer my questions. A soft wind blew across the sand in reply.

There was only one thing to do: only one way to find out what she was up to and where I might find her. I was going to have to read her diary again.

I felt bad doing it, and I sneaked aboard the boat feeling more like a burglar than ever, but the mystery was making me even more eager to find her.

The diary was in the locker. I opened it at the most recent entry. It was today's date!

Hooray! We're going to the Sunday market today! Father gave me extra pocket money. He says I can spend it on whatever I like. I've been saving all this month, so I'm hoping that I'll have enough for the dress I saw last time. I'm going to see if I can meet up with some of the girls from school.

A whole group of them have arranged to meet. They didn't actually invite me. I'm used to that. After letting them down so many times because of the tides or the weather doing the wrong thing, I don't blame them for giving up on me. Hopefully they won't mind me tagging along, though. And if I can't find them, there's always Richard from the year above us who works at the café at the back of the auction house. He smiled at me this week, and I'm sure he would have spoken to me if he hadn't been with his friends. Maybe he'll speak to me today.

I don't even know if I really like him. I hardly know him! But I'd rather have someone to talk to than wander around on my own all day. I'm desperate to have some fun. I can't remember the last time I laughed. It's been a hard month. People are saying it's the worst February they can recall, with all the bad weather we've had. I've missed ten days of school because of it.

I hope it will get better now. And I hope I'll have a wonderful time at the market. I'm sure I *will! See you later, diary. I'll come back later and tell you all about my day.*

Love,

D

I stared at the page, tracing the date with my finger. It was definitely today's date. And she definitely sounded like she had come to the market. Maybe she hadn't realized it had been canceled, after all. Which meant she was around somewhere — but where? And if she *was* here with her friends, would I really have the nerve to butt in and introduce myself?

I sat on the side of the boat and tried to figure out how I was going to make contact with her, while Flake ferreted around the crab pots.

And then I had a thought. Probably a very bad thought, but once it had come into my mind I couldn't get it out.

There was a black pen hooked onto a thin leather ring on the spine of the book. Without stopping to think about the ins and outs of it too much, I took the pen and opened the book at the first blank page. Then I looked around.

Should I?

Before I had time to talk myself out of it, I started writing.

Hi, Dee.

I hope you don't mind me calling you Dee. It feels like more of a name than just "D," and I don't know your real name.

I _really_ hope that you don't mind me writing in here, but I saw the book and it's so beautiful that I couldn't resist taking a look. I haven't read lots of it—I know it's private—but I happened to notice a little tiny bit, and you seem like the kind of girl I'd like to be friends with. I've got no one to talk to while I'm here at my gran's, and it sounds like you haven't got all that many people to talk to either—so I just sort of, kind of, wondered if maybe you'd like to hang out, perhaps?

If you do want to, you could maybe write me a note in here and we could arrange to meet up? That would be so cool! I'd love to meet up with you. It would be the first time I've actually made friends with someone here!

Anyway, I'll stop there. Once again, I'm really sorry for writing in your book. I hope you don't mind. (I happened to notice you said you believed you could write anything in a book as special as this. I thought exactly the same thing!!!!!!!)

Well, hope to meet up with you soon.

Mia

I read through what I'd written. Was it OK? Was it enough? Was it too much?

There was nothing I could do about it now, so I closed the diary, shoved it back in the locker, and got up.

"Come on, Flake. Let's go and throw some sticks."

Flake jumped up as soon as I said his name, and we climbed off the boat and headed back through the archway.

The second we were back on the beach, Flake stopped in his tracks. Slowly wagging his tail, he stared across the sand. I followed his gaze and spotted someone at the other end of the beach with a little white terrier.

Flake watched the person throw something for the dog — and that was his cue. He was off.

"Flake, come back!" I yelled, but he was already halfway across the beach, and a minute later, he and the terrier were running around, chasing each other in big yappy circles.

I kept calling him, and he kept ignoring me. Finally,

I caught up with them. The other dog's owner was a boy in jeans and a big woolly sweater. He was tall and gangly with a mop of dark hair that flopped over his forehead. He looked a couple of years older than me.

He glanced up as I approached. "Sorry — my dog seems to have stolen your dog," he said with an apologetic smile.

I smiled back and pointed to the stick in Flake's mouth. He was trotting around in circles, teasing the terrier with his catch. "Yeah, but my dog seems to have stolen your dog's stick!"

The boy laughed and we watched the dogs play. The terrier was trying to get the stick from Flake. He was about half Flake's size and kept jumping up at the stick, yapping constantly.

"Mitch, stop barking!" the boy said.

"Flake, give Mitch his stick back!" I added.

The dogs ignored both of us.

After a while, Flake seemed to get bored of the game and he dropped the stick, came over to me, and sat at my feet, wagging his tail.

I turned to the boy as I patted Flake. "I guess that's my cue to go," I said.

"See you around, then," he replied, and I turned to

leave. "My name's Peter, by the way," he called, and I turned back around. "We got here on Friday. We're on a fishing vacation."

"A fishing vacation? I didn't know they did those here."

I didn't know they did *anything* here, actually.

"Apparently, it's the first one they've done," Peter said.

"Sounds thrilling," I told him. "Poor you!"

Peter grinned. "No, it's great. I'm loving it. I caught six mackerel yesterday!"

If it weren't for the way Peter's eyes were shining, I'd have sworn he was being sarcastic. Could catching a bunch of fish really make someone smile that much? Could he honestly think that a fishing vacation in the back end of nowhere was great?

"Look—that's our boat," he said. He was pointing at a small boat in the harbor with fenders dangling all the way along the sides and a small wheelhouse in the middle. It looked just like Dee's dad's boat. For a moment, I actually wondered if it was the same one, but this one had a big outboard motor on it, and the registration number was SZ2965. Dee's boat was PN something.

The boat was lying slightly tilted in the sand. The harbor was half filled with water, but not enough to get the boat afloat yet.

"We're just waiting for the tide to come in, and then we're off," Peter said. He looked at his watch. "It's high tide at one twenty-seven today, so we should get afloat by about ten thirty."

I looked at him. He sounded like the fishermen around here. They were all obsessed with things like the tides. My grandad was the worst. He always had a tide table with him. He even had a clock in the pub that told you how far in or out the tide was, rather than telling you the actual time.

I couldn't see what there was to get all that excited about, to be honest. I was about to say so when Peter continued on. "They said we could try for sea bass today."

He looked at me, eyes all shiny and excited. I was probably supposed to say something that showed I was equally excited. I opened my mouth to reply, but couldn't think of anything. I mean, if he'd said, "They're opening a new multiplex theater on the edge of town, and some friends and I are planning to see a movie and go bowling," I would have understood why he looked so pleased. But fishing for sea bass? *Really?*

"Good luck with it," I managed eventually. I smiled as warmly as I could. I didn't want to put him off. He seemed really friendly and nice.

It was weird; he wasn't like the boys I knew back home. For one thing, none of the boys in my class would have known a mackerel from a sea bass if they'd been slapped across the face with the pair of them. But it was more than that. Whenever I talked to a boy back home — especially one a couple of years older than me, as Peter clearly was — I always clammed up and went all red in the face and felt like a complete and utter klutz. But I didn't feel like that with Peter. I felt — I don't know — comfortable, I guess.

Which was probably why I said what I said next.

"I'd love to go out on one of those boats sometime."

As soon as the words were out of my mouth, I wanted to chase after them and shove them back in. First of all, I instantly realized that it must have sounded like I was flirting with him, and I really wasn't. I mean, he wasn't bad looking or anything, and like I said, he seemed really nice — but nice in a big brother kind of way. The nice big brother I never had, as opposed to the grumpy, sullen one I did.

And secondly, because I could honestly say that I had never, not once, ever, in my entire life had the tiniest, remotest, incy-winciest desire to go out on the sea in a little fishing boat.

"Cool! Hey, I can ask if you could join us one day if you like?" Peter said with a wide smile.

"Awesome!" my mouth replied, without asking permission from my brain. But then, when I thought about it, why not? What else was there to do? His strange enthusiasm must have been infectious, because I actually had a moment of thinking that maybe it *could* be fun, in a sickly, wobbly, scary, fish-smelly kind of way.

Flake and Mitch were running around in circles again. "I'd better be getting back, then," Peter said. "Hey, what's your name?"

"Well, my real name's Amelia, but my friends call me Mia."

"Cool! I'd love to have a real name and another one that everyone called me!" He grinned. "I'll call you Mia, then. Have a good day — and I'll ask about the fishing trip."

"Great, yes, do that!" I replied. And even though I could hardly believe it, I actually meant it!

I headed back to the pub, Flake trotting along beside me, his tail wagging happily as he walked — and for the first time since we'd arrived, I understood how he felt.

* * *

Except, that all changed when we got back to the pub.

"Mom? Gran?" I called, and my voice echoed around the kitchen. I hung up Flake's leash and went through to the lounge.

They were sitting at a table. Gran had her head in her hands; Mom had an arm around her shoulders.

"Gran, what is it? Has something happened?" I asked, rushing over to join them.

Instantly, Gran lifted her head up, pulled back her hair, and sat up a bit straighter. Then she did this weird thing with her face, which I was fairly certain was supposed to be a smile, but looked more like the kind of expression you make when you're trying to eat something that tastes disgusting, but you don't want to offend the person who cooked it.

"Nothing's happened, dear. I'm fine," she said, reaching out to pat my hand. Then she did the smiling-through-gritted-teeth thing again, and added, "Did you have a nice walk?"

I paused for a moment before replying. It was *obvious* she wasn't fine. Why would she never talk to me properly? I could handle it. *I* wanted to know what had happened to Grandad, too. She wasn't the only one who was worried.

I wanted to say all these things. I even opened my mouth and felt my heart jump into it as I prepared myself to do so. But the words wouldn't come.

Instead, I found myself saying, "Yeah, lovely, thanks. Should I put the teakettle on?"

Mom gave me a grateful smile that just made me even more upset. "That would be lovely, darling."

So I went into the kitchen to make tea for three. And then we sipped our tea and pretended that everything was absolutely fine.

And for the rest of the day, that's pretty much all we did. Pretend. Gran pretended to be OK. I pretended not to be bored out of my skull. Mom pretended to be oblivious to all the pretending that was going on. And the minutes ticked by very slowly.

Monday morning, I woke up thinking about the boat and the diary and Dee. Would she have seen my note? Would we get to meet up? Maybe we'd become really good friends and she'd come and visit us back home — and I'd be a bit happier about coming to Porthaven more often.

We'd made breakfast for the three couples who were staying in the guest rooms. Gran was doing dishes. Mom was drying the dishes and chatting about anything she could think of that didn't involve the enormous elephant in the room that we all kept squeezing past and pretending wasn't there — i.e., the fact that Grandad still hadn't shown up or gotten in touch or *anything.*

It was time to get out of here.

"I'm just taking Flake out for a walk," I said, unhooking his leash. At the sound of the "w" word, Flake leaped from his bed in a flash, sitting upright and wagging his tail.

"You're very eager to walk the dog again," Mom observed.

"What's wrong with that?" I replied, perhaps a bit too sharply. Why did I feel guilty? It wasn't as if I was doing anything wrong — as long as you don't include the minor fact of boarding a boat that wasn't mine and reading the personal diary of someone I'd never even met.

Mom laughed. "Nothing at all. It's nice that you want to be so helpful, isn't it, Gran?"

Gran looked up from the dishes. She glanced vaguely at me. "Yes, it's very kind, thank you, dear," she said in a dull voice. And even though I totally understood that she wasn't herself because she was so worried about Grandad, and it was mean of me to even think it, I wanted to shake her and shout, "Talk to me! Be honest with me! Tell me how you feel — it won't kill you!" But there was too much of a gulf between us, full of all the words that we were too scared to say out loud. So I didn't try to get across it. Instead, I buttoned up my coat and hooked Flake's leash on to his collar.

"See you later, then," I said, and we went out into the cold.

The boat was there. I had a little flip of nerves in my stomach as we went down the jetty. Flake leaped on board as though it were our own boat, and I felt another twinge of guilt. But the desire to see if there was a reply to my note outweighed the guilty feeling.

I clambered onto the boat and pulled the back locker open. The diary was there. Before I had time to stop and think about it, I grabbed the book and opened it up.

And then I read eleven words that made my excitement plummet like a heavy anchor dropping to the bottom of the sea.

Who are you, and why are you reading my PRIVATE diary???

I looked around to see if I was being watched. I couldn't see anyone. I looked back at the page and read the words again. My face burned with shame. Now what?

I paused for a moment, and then I did the only thing I could think of doing.

I grabbed the pen, turned over the page, and started writing.

Vera

"One more step. Careful, now. The ground's quite bumpy. I don't want you to trip."

The man shifted the weight of the baby he was carrying in a sling on his chest. Holding on tightly to his wife's hand, he guided her as she gingerly put her left foot out and took the final step.

Vera laughed. "I hope this is going to be worth it when I open my eyes," she said.

"It will be," her husband replied, smiling. "You'll see." Then he turned her slightly to the right, and was about to undo the scarf he'd wrapped around her eyes.

Suddenly, he was nervous. What if she didn't feel the same way as he did about it? What if she couldn't see its potential? What if this wasn't the life she wanted for them all?

He hesitated.

"Frank, what is it?" she asked. "Are we there yet?" She could hear the sea lapping gently toward them and then softly receding, sucking the pebbles away with it. It was so close; they must be right at the water's edge.

At the sound of his wife's soft, questioning voice, Frank shook himself. He undid the scarf, and then, his voice shaking and low, he said, "Open your eyes."

Vera blinked a couple of times. The sun was bright, and her eyes had been covered with a scarf for the last twenty minutes.

She looked at the building in front of her. Two stone walls jutted forward, like arms reaching out toward her. In between them, weeds and grass and heaven knows what else was growing wild and free — almost as high as the top of the walls.

Behind the wildness was a blue door, its paint peeling from every panel, with rusty hinges and a stone arch over the top and, above that, a wooden window frame and a pointy roof with a chimney poking up from the side.

"I don't understand," she said. She turned to look at her husband. He was digging into his lip with a thumbnail. He always did that when he was nervous.

Vera reached out to him. She took his shaking hand and held it tight. Holding his hand tenderly against her cheek, she leaned forward to kiss their baby girl on her head. Only twenty or thirty steps from where they stood, the sea gently stroked the beach.

"Why are we here?" she asked. "What's going on?"

Frank hesitated. They had been here so often; they'd talked about it, shared their fantasies of the future. But maybe it wasn't what she wanted in real life. Maybe it had been just a game.

There was only one way to find out.

"It's our new home," he said. He couldn't look at her. What was he thinking? It was little more than a run-down shed. He was a fool! He was a —

"Really?" Vera was looking at him with shiny, wide eyes. "Really?"

Frank nodded.

And then her arms were around him. She was laughing, kissing him, jumping up and down. "You've made me the happiest girl in the world!"

All at once, the breath he felt as though he had been

holding since they'd arrived on the island came out in a rush, almost a sob.

He held his wife and his daughter as tightly as he could. Wrapped them up in all the love he had, tied together with his hopes for the future. They were going to build their life here. Here in this tiny village. He'd bought them a home — and she loved it!

Vera closed her eyes and felt the happiness wash over her like a sun-kissed wave. Their life as a family had truly begun.

Chapter Five

Monday, February 18

Dear Dee,

First of all, I need to apologize. I really am
sorry for reading your private diary. You must
think I'm a terrible person. Well, even if you don't,
I do. I've never done anything like it before. I'm
the girl who doesn't get into trouble at school
because I'm too chicken to do anything really
bad. I'm the girl who doesn't get yelled at at home
because I'd rather keep my mouth shut than do
anything to cause trouble. Seriously—I'm a good
person!

But, I suppose I'm also the girl who can't resist a mystery, and when I saw your boat, and the book kind of almost fell out of the locker (OK, that's not strictly true. It didn't fall out—but I could see it really clearly when the locker door fell open. And that's how honest I am—I can't even lie about something like that!!!), well, I was intrigued, I admit it.

Oh, and the only reason I was on the boat in the first place was because my gran's dog took a liking to the crab pots on the deck, and I had to get on board just to get him back. And I promise that's true!

So what I'm saying is, basically, I'm sorry. Please forgive me. Please?

I'd like to be your friend. I'm here to see my gran, who is going through a major crisis (I won't bore you with the details, but, trust me, it's a bad time), and I don't know anyone in the town except for Gran and my mom. You are literally the first person I've come across here who I could be friends with. Well, apart from a boy I met yesterday—but boys are different. You're the first one who seems just like me and who I think would totally understand me.

Like, the thing about the seals—I would have been SOOOOOOO excited to see that. I LOVE animals. I don't tell many people that, because, now that I'm almost in high school, it's not cool anymore. But I can tell you, because I know you'll understand. I think I'd like to be a vet when I grow up. What about you? (Oh, I've just realized—I've confessed that I read the part about the seals, too. I'm really sorry—again!)

Anyway, if you don't want to be friends, then just write another note like the last one (which was pretty scary, by the way!) and I'll leave you alone. But if you do want to be friends, then write to me in here.

I'll keep my fingers crossed.

Your friend (I hope),

Mia

Tuesday, February 19, 7:00 a.m.

Dear Mia,

I'd like to just get something clear before we go any further. This IS my private diary, and I DO think you were wrong for reading it. I'm not sure that I totally forgive you for that yet, but perhaps I will let it go. _For now._

I can't even believe I've just said that. My mother once glanced at a page of it, and I didn't speak to her for TWO WHOLE DAYS! That's how seriously I take it.

But from your note to me, well, I think that perhaps I feel differently about you reading it from how I felt when Mother did. I think what I'm saying is that I agree with you — you do sound a bit like me. You love animals, you say things the same way I do. And OK, in my heart of hearts, I admit it — if I'd seen the diary, I think I might have let my curiosity get the better of me, too.

Which DOESN'T mean that it's OK. OK?

It just means I understand.

And yes, you're right about the other thing, as well. The friends thing. Have you got a best friend? I have two good friends — Angela and Lydia — but I can't honestly call either of them my _best_ friend. They both live on the mainland, and that means they get to meet up a lot more often with each other than with me, so I end up being left out a lot.

I live in Luffsands (which you probably know already, depending on exactly how much of my diary you read!).

It's the island that's about two miles north of the mainland. You can see it from Porthaven on a clear day. You can't see the village, as it's on the opposite side of the island. The rest of the island is mainly woods and beaches. There are a few houses dotted around, but ours is the only village.

It's a bit similar to Porthaven, only even smaller. We have a grocery store, a tiny pub, a harbor, and about seventy houses. Most of the people who live here are fishing families. The only problem is, none of them include anyone my age. There are a couple of younger children. The Moss family has four-year-old twins, Molly and Jason. They live in a house right down near the beach, which they painted bright pink earlier this year because Molly wanted them to!

There are a couple of families with babies, and a few with older children, but the children moved off the island as soon as they were old enough. And as for girls my age — not a one! So it's pretty lonely.

Which is the ONLY reason why I have forgiven you for reading my diary!

Anyway, write back. I'm not coming across to the mainland for school this week, because it's spring break, but I'll sneak my diary onto the boat so my father can bring it over to you without even knowing!

Looking forward to hearing back from you,

Dee (I like the nickname, by the way — maybe I'll adopt it!)

Tuesday, February 19, 3:00 p.m.

Dear Dee (glad you like the name!),

I'm SOOOOOOOOOOO glad you wrote back to me. I've practically bitten my nails off, I've been so nervous. I had visions of you calling the police and having me carted off and arrested for trespassing! Thank you for forgiving me. What I did was pretty bad — but now that I've heard back from you, I'm really happy I did! (And really sorry, as well, obviously.)

I think your village sounds great. Maybe I could visit it one day this week. Or you could come over here. Don't you have any plans to come across to the mainland at all, even though it's spring break?

I'd ask my gran about coming to see you, but she's really preoccupied at the moment. My grandad has disappeared. It's all pretty awful, actually. They had an argument and he just went. It's been four days now. She hasn't told the police yet, but Mom phoned Dad today, and he says that if we still haven't heard anything by the end of today, then we have to call them tomorrow morning.

I know that he wouldn't just up and leave. I wish he'd get in touch and tell us where he is. Tell us he's fine. Just tell us <u>something</u>. I haven't said this to anyone yet, because Mom and Gran have got enough on their plates already, but the truth is, I'm really scared. I love my grandad. He's so kind and warm and friendly, and I just don't want anything to happen to him.

I can't talk to Gran about it — she doesn't talk about feelings at the best of times, but this week she's worse than ever. She's like one of those mussels that you can't open because they're completely sealed up.

Gosh, sorry. I don't know why I'm telling you all this. I don't even know you.

Thanks for listening anyway! Are you having

a nice week? What do you do in Luffsands during spring break?

Love,

Mia xxx

Wednesday, February 20, 6:45 a.m.

Dear Mia,

Oh, golly, how awful. I was so sad to read about your grandfather disappearing. That's terrible. Has he come back yet? I agree with your father. You should definitely call the police if he isn't back today.

Spring break in Luffsands is about helping Mother with her chores. She's a dressmaker and is always busy. I'm not very good at sewing, so she gives me the easy parts, where there are no complicated stitches required!

I like bird-watching, too. I've been watching the cormorants on the rocks just off the eastern tip of the island. There are hundreds of them at the moment. I think there must be some very interesting fish visiting us, to create so much interest!

Also, there's a fox who has been coming into our garden. He comes closer and closer each day to

pick at the crumbs I've been putting out for him.
My ambition is to feed him from my hand by the
end of the week. We'll see!

I bet I sound really boring!

What else have you been doing this week? I
hope your grandfather is home.

Oh, I nearly forgot! I think we'll be coming to
Porthaven on Friday! You know the annual fair?
After Christmas, it's the high point of the winter.
Will you still be there? Maybe we could meet?
That would be fun.

Maybe see you on Friday, then.

Dee

Wednesday, February 20, 2:30 p.m.
Dear Dee,

Hooray! Finally, some good news! I'm going
to meet you! I can't wait! We'll definitely still be
here. We're planning to stay at least till Sunday,
but if we still haven't heard anything and Grandad
still isn't back, we might even stay longer. Mom's
thinking about contacting my school to ask if I can
get special leave to miss the first few days back,
just in case.

I hope that doesn't happen, though. I mean, it's not that I'm crazy about school or anything. Normally, I'd jump for joy at the thought of no school for a few days—but not if it means that my grandad still isn't here.

The atmosphere is getting really bad. Gran normally doesn't show her feelings, but even she is finding it hard now. This morning I walked into the kitchen to see her in my mom's arms. Gran's shoulders were shaking. She didn't say anything, but Mom looked up and saw me and just kind of shook her head, so I left them alone. I don't think Gran would want anyone to know she'd been crying.

She called the police today. That's probably what set her off. When she did that, I think we all finally admitted that there was a problem. Up to now, we've been able to convince ourselves that he just needed a bit of a break, or that he's playing some silly game because they had an argument. But now that the police are involved, I suppose we all have to face up to the fact that it's really true. My grandad has gone missing—and he may never come back.

The police have put out calls and they've told us to leave it with them for now—which means we all feel even more useless than we felt before. All we can do is wait. It's horrible.

Sorry. What a miserable message. I hope you're having a better day — and my fingers and toes are all crossed for meeting up on Friday. That's the only thing I've got to look forward to.

Love,

Mia xx

Thursday, February 21, 6:50 a.m.

Oh, Mia, I'm so sorry to hear all this bad news. It makes me want to meet up even more, as I think it sounds like you need a friend there more than anything.

I'm not going to write much, as Father is about to leave and I don't want to miss getting this message to you. I want you to know I'm thinking about you, and I really, really, really, really, really hope your grandfather is home by the time you read this.

We're definitely coming to the fair — as long as the weather is good enough for us to get there. There's a storm predicted for tomorrow, so I'm hoping the weathermen are wrong. They usually are, aren't they?

I'll come with Father in the morning. Shall we meet at the harbor and then we could go together? Let's meet by the arches at, say, ten o'clock?

Oh, what do you look like? I'm about average height for my age — which is thirteen, by the way. How old are you? I have shoulder-length auburn hair, with a cowlick at the front (I've tried a million ways to stop it from sticking out, but no luck!), and green eyes, and I'll be wearing a brown suede jacket and probably a skirt with rain boots. It's not the most stylish look in the world, but it's practical.

Till tomorrow — I hope! I'm getting excited.

Your friend,

Dee

Thursday, February 21, 1:39 p.m.

I'm excited too!

OK, so, I'm thirteen, medium sort of height, very skinny. I've got blond hair, a bit longer than yours. Wait . . . OK, I just measured. If I stand straight, with my arms by my sides, my hair comes to about halfway between my shoulders and my elbows.

I'll be at the arches at ten a.m. I'll be wearing black jeans and a tan wool coat on top of lots of layers. It's really cold today!

Fingers crossed for the weather. It's calm today, so let's hope it stays like this.

See you in just over twenty hours! ☺

Your friend,

Mia

Chapter Six

Friday morning, I glanced at my watch for the fiftieth time. It was nearly ten o'clock. Gran hadn't even gotten out of bed, so Mom and I had been doing the breakfasts.

Everyone had eaten but there was still all the cleaning up to do. I didn't want to leave Mom to do it all on her own, and I had no idea when Gran was going to get up. Mom said we shouldn't disturb her. She hadn't been sleeping well since Grandad disappeared, so if she was actually managing to get some sleep now, the least we could do was let her rest.

I'd already walked Flake so I'd be free to meet up with Dee, but I was still running late.

"I just don't know what we're going to do about all this," Mom said. "I mean, we haven't heard anything useful from the police, and he's been gone a week now. I'm so worried."

"I know, Mom. I am too," I said. What else could I say? The police didn't know anything. Gran was hardly speaking to anyone. She walked around the place like a ghost. Mom was pretty much running the pub and she and I were cleaning the rooms.

For the first time in my life, I felt myself starting to get angry with Grandad. How could he do this? Didn't he care about any of us?

I refused — absolutely point-blank *refused* — to consider that anything terrible might have happened to him. That simply wasn't an option. So the only option left was to get angry with him.

I had to get out of there.

"Mom, could I . . . um, could I go out for a bit?" I asked hesitantly, once I'd finished stacking the dishwasher.

Mom turned to look at me. "Out?" she asked with such shock in her voice that for a second I actually wondered if I'd accidentally asked if I could fly to the moon on the back of a unicorn.

"Yes, it's just . . . I'm meeting a friend."

"Oh, yes. Of course." Mom smiled at me. Her eyes looked so tired.

"Mom, he'll come back," I said. I didn't know if I believed it, but I wanted to offer her some hope and I didn't have anything else.

"I'm sure he will, hon. You go out."

I kissed her on the cheek. "I won't be gone long. Thank you."

Then I grabbed my coat and ran as fast as I could down to the harbor.

Dee wasn't there.

In fact, no one was there at all. The beach was empty. Most of the fishing boats were out, so the harbor was practically empty, too. And the fair that was supposed to be going on all day — well, I could see a few people putting up a booth at the far side of the harbor, but it certainly didn't look like something that could qualify as the high point of the season.

I stood at the arches, waiting. She was probably just late.

But it was quarter past ten. *I* was the one who was late. Maybe she'd been here, but she'd gone off to look for me. Or maybe she'd just given up on me, decided I wasn't coming.

But then she'd have to be here *somewhere,* wouldn't she?

Maybe she and her dad hadn't come across to Porthaven at all.

I looked through the arches, but couldn't see to the other side. It was quite choppy, and mid-tide, and the water in the arches came halfway up my shins.

Good thing I'd followed Dee's lead and decided to wear my rain boots.

I rolled my jeans up and waded through the archway.

The boat was there! So Dee *was* here! But where?

Maybe she'd left me a note.

I approached the boat. It was bouncing around on the lapping waves. I gripped the side rails and hurled myself sideways into the boat.

I landed with a thump on the deck and looked around to make sure no one had seen my not-very-elegant maneuver.

Holding on to the rails, I stepped carefully along the deck to the back of the boat. Maybe she'd left a message for me, suggesting we meet somewhere else.

I opened the locker and pulled out her diary. There *was* a note from her.

Dear Mia,

I am SO disappointed. Father wouldn't bring me. He said that it's too rough to take me. I didn't think it was so bad, and we had an argument.

I never argue with my father, so you can imagine how upset I am. Not just because of that, but also because I wanted to meet up with you SO much. You are the nearest I've come to having a friend on truly the same wavelength, and now I'm not even going to meet you.

I am so upset. I cried after I argued with Father. He didn't see. He was too busy preparing the boat. Mother didn't want him to go out at all, but he said he has to go today. These big swells are the best for catching all sorts of rare varieties of fish that are normally beyond his reach. It's days like this that could make us rich, he said.

He kissed the anchor pendant he always wears around his neck and said he'd be fine. Mom gave him the pendant when they were courting, and he never goes fishing without it.

Then he assured us both that he would be careful, and all would be well. Which of course made me ask again why I couldn't go with him. But he wouldn't relent.

He said if it had been likely to improve later, he might have said yes, but it's due to worsen and he wasn't going to put me at risk.

Which of course made Mother insist that he not go out, either. So then <u>they</u> argued, too. What a terrible, awful day. Father is about to go off on angry seas, in an angry mood, Mother is upstairs crying, and I'm missing out on something I've looked forward to so much. Not just the fair, but my chance to meet someone who I feel sure could be a wonderful friend.

I'll slip the diary onto the boat as usual, and I hope you get it. I won't receive your reply till Father comes home this afternoon. I can't tell you how upset I am. I hope you aren't angry with me. That would just make a terrible situation even worse.

Your friend,
Dee

I scanned her note twice, just to make sure I'd read it correctly. She wasn't coming. I didn't have *anything* to look forward to. The one nice thing about this week—

the one possible thing that wasn't clouded in misery and sadness — wasn't happening.

I was too miserable to reply right away. I didn't want to share how upset I was; it would only make Dee feel worse. I decided I'd come back and reply later when I didn't feel quite so disappointed. The last thing she needed was a miserable note from me.

I left the diary on the boat and waded back under the archway. The tide was even higher now, and a wave hit me just as I was in the middle of the arch. The water went right over the top of my boots and soaked my feet and jeans.

And then it started raining.

Pulling on my hood, I hurried back to the beach. Head down, I squelched across the sand, trying to think of anything that wouldn't make me feel like curling up in a ball and bursting into tears, when something ran into my ankle.

I shoved my hood back and looked down. It was Mitch! He ran yapping and jumping around my legs.

I bent down to pet him and he flopped straight over onto his back.

"Mitch, you know you're drenched, don't you?" I asked as I tickled his tummy.

Mitch rolled back onto his feet. His back was

covered in sand; it was glued onto his fur like an extra layer.

"Hey, hi again!"

I looked up to see Peter coming toward me. "Hi," I replied. "Wow. Nice coat." I pretended to shade my eyes. He was wearing a bright-yellow waterproof coat, with a fluorescent white stripe across the middle and a "Porthaven Harbor" sticker on the pocket. It looked brand-new.

Peter beamed. "Dad got it for me yesterday. I love it. Almost slept in it last night."

I laughed. "How come you're not fishing today?"

"We will be later. It's going to be sunny this afternoon, apparently."

Sunny? But Dee said it was due to get worse. "Are you sure?"

Peter shrugged. "Well, despite my all-weather coat, I'm not a weatherman, so I can't be totally positive," he said with a wink. "But look." He pointed at the horizon. "The clouds are right above us now, but it's blue over there. And see the flag at the end of the pier? It's blowing toward us, so the wind's blowing that blue sky over here. Reckon it'll be lovely in an hour's time."

I stared at him. "Are you serious?"

"About what?"

"Well, you said you're not a weatherman, but you sound like one to me!"

Peter laughed. His laugh was so warm and friendly, it seeped into my mood and made me relax a bit. "It's the fishing lessons," he said. "They've been teaching us how to predict the weather. It's cool. You can tell so much, just from what the clouds look like."

"Uh-huh," I said.

Peter laughed again.

"What?"

He shook his head. "You just *uh-huh*'d me in the same way my sister does. I guess I'm the only one who finds this stuff interesting."

"No, sorry, it's not that. It *is* interesting."

Peter raised his eyebrows.

"OK, so it's not *that* interesting," I said, laughing. "But I'm just a bit preoccupied and miserable today, so I'm not finding anything particularly interesting."

"What's up?"

I looked at him. Normally, I'd just have said that everything was fine, and shrugged it off, especially with someone I barely knew. But there was something about Peter that made me want to talk to him. I didn't know what it was. I just felt comfortable with him, as though he was a friend I'd known all my life.

"You really want to know?" I asked.

Peter held my gaze. "I haven't got anything else to do for a couple of hours. Why don't you tell me your problems?"

And so I did. I told him everything. I told him about all the plans I'd had with my friends this week. I told him about Grandad disappearing, and how none of us were talking about how we really felt because we were all too scared to admit out loud how terrified we were.

And I told him about Dee, and how missing her felt like the last straw. I didn't tell him that I only knew her because I'd trespassed on her boat, but I told him that her dad's boat was moored up around the back of the arches.

As soon as he heard this, Peter's eyes lit up. "Really? I didn't realize anyone still used that old jetty," he said. "Can I see it?"

"I don't see why not. As long as you don't mind getting wet. The water's practically up to your knees under the arches."

Peter shook his head. "I don't mind that at all. Come on. Show me the boat."

So Peter picked up Mitch and we trudged back under the arch.

But the boat had gone.

"Wait—it was there! I saw it. I was *on* it!"

"Maybe Dee's dad has gone back," Peter said.

"But we'd have seen him, wouldn't we? We've been on the beach the whole time!"

"Maybe there's another way around here?"

"Oh, what does it matter anyway?" I said, turning to head back through the arch. "The point is, Dee's not coming. And all I've got to look forward to today is moping around with Mom and Gran at the pub, all of us jumping a mile in the air every time the door opens in case it's Grandad, and all of us pretending we're not disappointed every time it isn't."

I suddenly realized what a downer I was. We were back on the beach now. Peter put Mitch down and he immediately scampered off to chase some seagulls.

"Sorry," I said. "I'd better get going. Enjoy your fishing trip. See you later."

"Yeah, see you," Peter replied. "I hope your day gets better." Then he called Mitch back, and they walked off in the opposite direction.

As they went off, I realized I had another thing to be miserable about. Now that the boat had gone, I wouldn't get to reply to Dee's last note. How rude would that look? Dee would probably decide not to bother being my friend at all, now.

I dragged myself back to the pub and desperately tried — and dismally failed — to imagine anything good happening today.

The morning dragged so much that a couple of times I even checked my watch against the clock in the kitchen, to make sure it was still working. It was almost lunchtime and I was wiping down the tables in the pub. Mom and Gran were out back. The front door burst open.

My heart did the same leap in the air it had done every time someone came in — followed by the same sinking to the ground it did every time it wasn't Grandad.

It was Peter. "It's back!" he said breathlessly.

"What is?"

"The boat. The one behind the arches. I went back to the harbor to find out what time the fishing trip was, and it's been canceled — the boss is sick. Apparently he had some bad oysters last night and can't leave his house — or probably his bathroom, more like!"

"So you're not going out?"

Peter's eyes did that twinkly thing. "Well, not officially. But I have an idea."

"What?"

He tapped his nose conspiratorially. "Meet me

down at the harbor, and I'll tell you. But you've got to be up for an adventure."

Before I had time to answer, he was gone.

Gran came into the lounge a second later. "Was there someone here?" she asked. I could see the hope in her eyes. She was trying to hide it, but it was there, clouded with anxiety and fear.

"It was a friend of mine," I said. "We're just going to go out for a little while. Is that OK?"

The glimmer of hope in Gran's eyes dissolved into a dark veil of sadness. I wanted to reach out to her. I wanted to tell her that I cared, that I was here, that I understood. But I didn't know how to. We simply didn't have a common language. It wasn't her fault, or mine. We'd just never ever had anything in common. Until this week.

"Gran — he'll be back," I said. "I'm sure he will. And until then, Mom and I aren't going anywhere. Grandad is just as important to us as he is to you, and we're going to be with you till he comes back. We'll look after you."

The words came out in a rush, and I felt silly as soon as I'd uttered them. I knew Gran. She'd think I was an idiot for suggesting that I could look after her — for even thinking that she'd *want* me to!

But she looked me in the eyes. Then she came over

to me and touched my arm. "You're a good girl," she said softly. "You always have been. And you're very precious to us both. You know that, don't you?"

"I . . . I . . ." I'd *probably* known it. She'd never said it before, not like that — so how could I have known for sure? But I did now, and I wanted her to know I cared too. I leaned forward and put my arms awkwardly around her waist.

For a moment, she stiffened. Then I felt her relax. She put her arms around me, too, and patted my back. "All right, come on, now," she said after a moment. "Let's get on with the day. You go and see your friend. Have a nice time. Don't stay out too long, all right?"

"I won't," I said. And then I grabbed my coat and went out to join Peter and find out about his mystery plan.

Chapter Seven

"Peter, you're talking about theft!"

"It's not theft. I'm not going to *keep* it. We're just going to use it to fetch Dee. And it's her boat anyway!"

"It's her *dad's* boat."

"Same difference."

We were sitting on the boat, bobbing gently up and down. I bit my lip while I thought about it. Peter's plan was that we should take the boat and go to fetch Dee. He reckoned if it was only two miles to Luffsands, we could easily get there, pick her up, and be back here again within an hour or two. And the weather seemed to have turned out nice after all, so there was no real reason why she couldn't come with us.

"But what about her dad? What if he comes back and sees the boat's not here?" I asked.

"He won't. The auction's going on now. He's not going to leave till it's finished, is he? We can be there and back before he even comes down here again."

Peter had a point. The annual winter fair might have been a bit of a letdown, but the auction that went with it was rocking. We could hear the crowd shouting and bartering from the harbor.

"Are you absolutely sure you know how to drive this boat?"

"Positive!" Peter said. "The skipper said I'm the best he's ever seen. A complete natural. I picked it up on the first day and he's been letting me drive every day since then. He even left me in charge yesterday while he went to the back to help the others straighten out their lines. I'm totally comfortable with it. I might as well have been born doing it."

The excitement in Peter's eyes was infectious, but I still couldn't go along with it.

"It feels wrong," I said, a little more uncertainly.

"I know," he said. "I understand. And, believe me, this isn't the kind of thing I would normally suggest. But

Dee being stuck over there, miserable as anything, and you over here, equally miserable, feels just as wrong."

He had a point. How much harm could it really do? Dee's dad would never know, and we would absolutely make Dee's day. Her week. Once we'd cheered her up, she could make up with her dad and everyone would be happy again. We might, in fact, be doing the whole family a favor!

"We'd have to leave some money on the boat to cover fuel," I said.

"Of course we will!" Peter said. Then he grinned. "You mean, we're doing it?"

Were we? Could we, *really*? Despite my reservations, I couldn't help feeling a spark of excitement catch light inside me. I was going to meet my new friend. I felt as if I knew her already, and we hadn't even met yet! "What will Dee say to her dad to explain how she got here?" I asked.

Peter rubbed his chin. There was something about the way he did it that felt familiar to me, but I couldn't think why. It was weird; I'd honestly never felt so comfortable with a boy.

"Got it!" he exclaimed, grinning. "She can tell him that one of the other fishermen picked her up. They'll all have come in by now for the auction."

"Doesn't sound all that convincing to me, but I guess she might have some ideas. And if we can't think of anything, she doesn't even have to come back with us. I'll still have met her. That's the main thing."

"Exactly!" Peter said. "Look!" He pointed at the water. "It's totally calm. The weather's cleared up and so has the sea. Dee's dad was wrong about a storm. He'll probably be really pleased that she managed to get a lift across."

I hesitated before replying, and Peter leaped on my indecision. "I bet he even keeps the key in the same place as all the others," he said. He got up and lifted the mattress on his seat. There was a lid on the top of the bench, which he lifted as well. He felt around, then pulled out a cork ball with a key on the end of it.

"Ta-da!" he said, smiling broadly.

I couldn't help smiling back. His excitement was growing on me. Maybe he was right. Maybe we *could* do this.

"Mia — this could be your *only* chance to meet Dee," he said firmly.

I didn't need to be told that. That was the biggest thought in my mind. And he was right. What was the worst thing that could happen? Maybe Dee *would* have an argument with her dad about it, but the chances were they'd get to make up sooner, not later.

And the thought of her face when we turned up at Luffsands — I couldn't wait! Without letting myself think about it anymore, I nodded at Peter. "OK," I said. "Let's do it."

We slowly pulled away from the jetty, the boat gliding on the glassy water. It was so calm. The weathermen really *were* useless! Dee's dad had gotten it totally wrong.

We came gently around into the bay. Peter was in the wheelhouse, focusing ahead, and every now and then glancing at the compass. The wind was gentle on my face as I leaned back against the side of the boat and closed my eyes. It was blissful. I'd never felt so at peace, so relaxed, so excited, so —

"AMELIA!"

In a nanosecond I was upright in my seat, eyes wide-open.

"MIA!"

It was Mom! She was on the beach with Flake. She looked furious.

"Amelia, what are you doing?" she yelled.

"Mom, what's wrong?" I called.

"What's wrong?" she called back, running toward

the sea. "Your gran's world has fallen apart, I'm trying to hold the place together, and you're off joyriding on a boat with some strange boy we've never even laid eyes on before. What do you *think* is wrong?"

I glanced at Peter in the wheelhouse. He'd changed course and was steering us toward the jetty, closer to Mom. I didn't know if he'd heard what she'd said, but if he had, he was doing a good job of acting as though he wasn't offended.

"Look, we won't be out long," I began.

"You won't be out at *all*!" Mom snapped. "I don't know what you're thinking."

"I'm thinking I'm entitled to have at least one nice thing this week!" I snapped back. I didn't mean to, but — well, she wasn't the only one trying to cope with all this.

Mom just looked at me. "None of us is *entitled* to *anything* while your grandad is missing," she said.

We were nearly alongside the jetty now, and close enough that I could see Mom clenching her jaw and dark circles under her red eyes. She looked as if she'd aged a decade this week. That was when it hit me. It was her *dad* who had gone missing. However bad this was for me, it was fifty times worse for *her*. How could I be so selfish?

"Mom, I'm sorry," I said. "Just give me a minute." I opened the door to the wheelhouse. "We'll have to forget it," I said to Peter. "Nice idea, though."

Peter nodded. But his jaw was set, his eyes determined. "Look, I'll drop you off," he said, "but I'm going to fetch Dee for you."

"You can't go on your own. She doesn't even know you!"

"You've described her to me. I'll tell her I'm your friend. I'll explain everything."

I thought about it. The idea was tempting. I was desperate to meet up with Dee, and Peter could make it happen. But I couldn't convince my brain that it was the right thing to do. "Peter, you can't," I said.

"Why not?"

"Think about it. Dee has no idea who you are. She's not likely to go off on a boat with some boy she's never met. A boat that the boy has just stolen from her dad!"

"I'm not stealing—"

"*I* know you're not stealing, but it would be hard to convince anyone else you weren't. Dee's never heard of you, her dad's never met you, you have no link with this boat at all."

Peter let out a heavy breath. "When you put it like that . . ."

"You know I'm right. You really can't do it."

He nodded. "I guess."

"Peter, look at me."

He looked up. "What?"

"You really can't."

"OK. You're right. It's just a shame, though."

"Hey, you don't need to tell *me* that."

He steered the boat perfectly alongside the jetty and jumped off to tie the ropes around a cleat. I could see what the fisherman meant. Peter did the whole thing so quickly and so naturally it was as if he'd been doing it all his life.

He reached out to help me off the boat. "I'll take it back around to the old jetty," he said. "You go back with your mom."

"Promise me you won't go to Luffsands."

"I promise," he said. "See you tomorrow maybe." And with that, he quickly pulled the ropes off the cleat and jumped aboard again. "I'll leave the boat exactly where we found it," he called, giving me a quick salute and a lopsided grin. "I promise."

Mom put her arm around my shoulders as we walked back up to the beach. "I'm sorry, darling," she said. "I didn't mean to get so angry. It's just — when I saw you on the boat like that, I imagined something terrible happening to you. I can't lose you as well."

At that, her voice cracked and I wrapped an arm around her. "You're not losing *anyone*," I said fiercely.

She swallowed hard and wiped a hand across her cheek. "Thank you, sweetheart," she said. Then she linked her arm through mine. "Come on," she said. "Let's get back to your gran."

Back at the pub, Gran had made us some lunch. We ate in silence for a while.

Gran was the first to break it. "We need to pull ourselves together," she said, putting down her knife and fork and folding her arms. "We've got a pub to run. We've got lives to get on with. We need to have some faith, some belief. So I've decided. We're not going to worry anymore. We're to believe he'll come back. Agreed?"

"OK," I said.

"Agreed," Mom added. I got up and stood in between them, and the three of us joined arms. Soon we were hugging and smiling and holding on to one another just long enough to let each other know that, in our hearts, we didn't ever want to let go.

Frank

He pulled up to the jetty and moored up on the ring at the end. Slipping the key into its usual hiding place, he hauled his catch off the boat. It wasn't easy. The swell had raged earlier, but suddenly calmed somewhere along the way. He took that as a good sign.

The size of his catch was an even better sign. He couldn't remember the last time he'd had a run like this.

He'd argued with his wife and his daughter before he left home, but, oh, boy, he'd make it up to them when he got back. They'd have the finest oysters tonight. He'd buy them with the money he was about to earn at the auction.

Itching with anticipation, he carried his box around to the auction house. He marched straight up to the scales where the fishermen's catches were weighed in.

"Morning, Charlie—how about this, then?" Frank said, smiling as he heaved his box onto the scales. But as he looked up, the smile froze on his face. "You're not Charlie," he said.

"Who's Charlie?" the man at the weigh-in asked.

Frank laughed. "Who's Charlie? He's only worked here as long as I can remember!"

The man shrugged. "Weigh-in's been my job the last four years."

Frank stared at the man. Then he laughed again—only not quite so confidently this time. "Hey, it's a joke, isn't it?" he said.

The man stared back. "Do you want your catch weighed or not?"

Frank hesitated, mouth open. He couldn't think of anything to say. Eventually he nodded.

The man weighed Frank's fish and wrote a number on a piece of paper. "You'll be in auction number three," he said. "Starts at two. Good catch there, buddy."

As the man turned to his next customer, Frank stumbled away from the scales. What was going on? Where was Charlie?

He looked around the auction house, searching for a friendly face who could solve his puzzle — or tell him who the practical joker at the scales was.

But he couldn't see a friendly face. Well, no. That wasn't strictly true. The faces were friendly enough, just not familiar. Nearly fifteen years he'd been coming here, and he knew almost all the fishermen in the area. But not today.

He didn't recognize a single one.

Frank stumbled to the benches at the back of the auction house. He sat down, pulled out a handkerchief, and wiped his forehead. It was dripping with sweat; his hands were shaking.

What was going on? Why didn't he know anyone?

What was wrong with him?

Chapter Eight

Saturday morning I was wide-awake before Mom or Gran or any of the guests. After tossing and turning for half an hour, I got up and sneaked downstairs. Flake wagged his tail lazily when he saw me.

"Come on, let's go out," I said, grabbing his leash. Then I quietly opened the back door and we set off down to the harbor.

Flake ran happily up and down the beach, chasing seagulls and barking at the waves. Every now and then he'd pick up a stick and bring it to me, dropping it at my feet and wagging his tail. I threw the stick distractedly and moseyed over to the old jetty. Maybe, by some miracle, Dee would be coming today. Or there might be another note, at least. The more I thought about it, the more I convinced myself it was possible. I desperately wanted it to be. Apart from anything else, I wanted the chance to reply to her last note and explain why I hadn't replied yesterday.

I ducked down to get through the arches. The water was up to my ankles and the bottom of my jeans got soaked, as I'd forgotten to tuck them into my boots. I hardly noticed. All I cared about now was seeing the boat.

But it wasn't there.

Well, of course it wasn't. For one thing, it was about seven o' clock in the morning. And for another, it was Saturday. Dee's dad was as entitled to his weekend off as anyone else.

By the time I got back to the pub, I knew I had to shake myself out of my miserable mood. It wouldn't be fair to Mom and Gran if I spent all weekend moping around, so I decided I was going to be helpful and cheerful instead. Well, cheerful might be a bit too much to ask, but it wouldn't do any harm to try.

So I tidied up my room, and then I cleaned the kitchen, and by the time I'd done that and helped with the breakfasts, I'd managed to pass a couple of hours.

Part of me wanted to go down to the harbor again, just in case. But I knew it was pointless. Dee wouldn't be coming. Distraction was definitely my best strategy.

"Mom, is there anything I can do?" I asked when I'd run out of things that obviously needed attending to. Gran was upstairs cleaning the guest rooms and Mom was in charge of the pub. There was hardly anyone in, just a couple of fishermen sitting on the tall stools at the bar.

"You could collect some glasses."

"There aren't any."

"Oh. Wipe the counters?"

"Done it already," I said.

Mom looked around the bar and shook her head. "Well, darling, I can't really think of anything else. Haven't you got anything to do? Why don't you meet up with one of your new friends?"

Yeah. Sore point, Mom.

But then I had a thought. Maybe there *was* a way I could meet up with Dee, after all.

"Mom, we're not likely to be really busy in the pub today, are we?" I asked.

Mom looked around the almost empty room and laughed. "I very much doubt it, somehow."

"So, why don't we see if Gran will close up for a few hours and take a trip out?"

Mom looked at me. "A trip out? All three of us?"

I nodded.

"Where would you like to go?"

I paused and tried to look as if I were having a good think. "Oh, I don't know," I said. "Maybe we could go on a boat trip or something."

"I never knew you liked boats so much," Mom said. "You must get it from your grandad."

"Mm," I replied.

"I suppose I did stop you from taking a boat trip yesterday, and it might be good for your gran. Anything's got to be better than moping around here all day, waiting for something to happen."

"Exactly!"

"So, where do you have in mind?" Mom asked.

I took a deep breath, tried to ignore the thumping, racing feeling in my chest, and said as casually as possible, "I dunno. Luffsands, maybe?"

At which point, for some reason, one of the fishermen who had been sitting in silence for the last ten minutes suddenly spurted his beer all over the bar.

"Oh!" Mom exclaimed, and ran out to get a towel.

As the door swung closed behind her, the fisherman raised his glass to me. "Good luck with that one," he said, with a twinkle in his eye. He seemed to be laughing at me.

"Think you might want to come up with another idea," his friend added. "Somewhere that—how can I put it—actually still exists?"

Then the two of them both fell forward, laughing and slapping each other on the back.

Before I had a chance to reply, the door at the back of the bar opened and Mom came back in with a towel.

Gran was behind her. "What's happened here?" she asked as Mom wiped up the beer.

I opened my mouth to answer, but one of the men beat me to it. "We were just talking about the power of the sea," he said, with a wink.

Gran raised an eyebrow and looked at me. "Well, whatever it is they've been telling you, don't listen to a word of it," she said good-humoredly. "These men are the biggest storytellers I've ever known. They'd catch a tadpole and tell you it was a shark. Now, what can I get you?"

And with that, Gran poured the men a pint each and the conversation was over and forgotten.

I didn't know what the men had meant, but I was sure Gran was right about them. Most of the customers in this place talked nonsense at least half the time, especially when they had a drink in their hands.

I was about to ask Gran what she thought of my idea about going out, when a customer asked for a cup of tea and she went into the kitchen to boil the teakettle. As she went out, the front door opened and a family came in: a man, a woman, and a girl who looked about my age. They stood awkwardly just inside the door and didn't make a move to come in any farther.

"Brunch, is it?" Mom asked, wiping her hands on a towel. "Table for three?"

"Er, we were just . . ." the woman began. Her voice trembled and she broke off and bit her lip.

The man took a step forward. "We're looking for the owner," he said. "Is that you?"

"It's my mother," Mom said. "I'll tell her you want to see her."

Mom disappeared into the kitchen and left me with the family. I was going to leave them to it, but I was intrigued. The three of them were standing there in silence, not coming in, just waiting for Gran. Who were they? What did they want? Was it something to do with Grandad?

My heart took a tiny tumble with the thought, but I forced myself not to believe it could be possible.

I smiled at them, and we all waited awkwardly, not knowing what to say.

Thankfully, Mom came back a moment later. "She won't be but a minute," she said. "Can I get you anything while you're waiting?"

The man shook his head. "We're OK, thanks."

I watched him as he spoke. There was something familiar about him. I didn't recognize the woman, and I was pretty sure I hadn't seen the girl before, although, in all honesty, it was hard to tell, as she'd been looking down at her feet since they'd come in. But I could have sworn I recognized the man from somewhere. Maybe he was famous.

"Have I seen you before?" I asked him.

He looked back at me, confusion brushing across his face. "I don't think so," he said. "Sorry, I'm . . . we're . . ."

Just then, Gran came back. She delivered the cup of tea to the customer at the bar and smiled her bright "pub owner" smile at the family as she came into the lounge. It was easy to see where Mom and I both got our pretend smiles from.

"Hello, I'm the owner," she said as she picked up a couple of glasses from a table to take back to the bar. "How can I help you?"

The woman reached into her bag. "We wondered if we could ask you a favor," she said. "We'd like to put something up on your bulletin board, if you have one. Or perhaps in your window?"

"Well, I don't usually . . ." Gran began. "What is it?"

The woman pulled out a sheet of paper. "It's our . . . our . . . " Then she swallowed hard and stopped.

The man reached out to hold her hand. He cleared his throat. "It's our son," he said soberly. "He's gone missing."

"Oh, you poor things," Gran said. "Of course you can."

The woman held out the piece of paper. Gran went over to take it from her. And then something weird happened.

Gran looked at the piece of paper. Her smile froze. Her hand stiffened. The paper fell from her hand. The glasses in her other hand fell, too.

As the glasses hit the floor, Gran looked as though she'd been punched, and she staggered back to lean on a table.

I rushed over. "Gran, are you OK?"

Mom was on her knees, picking up chunks of glass, apologizing to the woman. The couple had stepped back and was looking from Mom to Gran. Gran was leaning heavily on the table, staring into space and breathing hard.

"I'm fine," she said breathlessly.

Mom looked up at me. "Grab the dustpan, please," she said.

I ran into the kitchen to get the dustpan and brush. As I came back through to the lounge, I ran smack-dab into Gran coming the other way.

"Gran, where are you going?" I asked.

She paused for a second and shook her head. "Just give me a minute, Amelia," she said.

I let her pass and went into the lounge.

"Gran's not been well," I said to the family. "She's got a lot going on at the moment."

The woman had picked up her piece of paper and was holding it against her chest, as though protecting it. She must have thought we were all crazy. I wouldn't blame them if they didn't want us to have anything to do with them *or* their son.

I passed the brush and pan to Mom and pointed to a table near the bar. "Look, why don't you just sit down here for a moment?" I said to the family. "Gran'll be back in a sec. I'll grab you a drink."

The woman nodded. "Tea would be lovely. Thank you, dear."

I turned to the man.

"I'll have a coffee, thanks," he said.

The girl looked up briefly. "Can I have a Coke, please?" she said quietly.

"Coming right up," I said as cheerfully as I could — which, to be fair, wasn't cheerfully at all. But I don't think anyone noticed.

I went back into the kitchen and put the kettle on. While it was boiling, I got two cups out and filled a glass with Coke.

I listened to the kettle fizzle and squeak as it warmed up, and I tried to make sense of what had just happened to Gran. Why had she lost it like that? Was she sick? Was it the stress of everything? But why then?

And then I realized. Of *course* she'd be upset. Some people had come through the door who had just lost someone — and so had she! It was *bound* to upset her.

I left the kettle to boil and went upstairs to find her.

She wasn't in her bedroom. I checked mine and Mom's, and she wasn't in either of those.

Then I heard a sound coming from the floor above. There was just one room up there. Grandad called it his study, but it was a junk room, really. He was the only one who ever used it. I hadn't been in there for years. As far as I knew, Gran never went in there. She always said she couldn't bear the mess.

But she was in there now.

"Gran?" I called uncertainly from the landing.

She didn't reply. I climbed a few stairs and called again. "Gran, are you up there?"

This time, I heard something that sounded like a box toppling over, followed by Gran's voice. "You stupid, stupid man!" she said. Who was she talking to? *Was Grandad in there?*

I ran to the top of the stairs and stood in the doorway. At first I couldn't even see her. All I could see was boxes piled on top of one another, overflowing bags scrunched in between them all, mess strewn everywhere. If I didn't know what Grandad was like, I'd have sworn we'd been burgled.

Then I spotted Gran sitting in the middle of the room, cross-legged, with a bag of photographs on her knee. She was clutching her left foot.

She looked up at me and tried to smile, but there was a big black mascara mark running down her cheek in a wiggly line, which didn't do much to convince me the smile was real.

She must have seen me staring, as she quickly

looked away and rubbed her sleeve across her face. When she looked back, the wiggly line had turned into a big black splotch. It looked as if she'd smeared a lump of coal across her cheek.

I picked my way through the mess and sat down beside her. "Gran, what happened?" I asked gently.

"Darn box fell on my toe," she said, trying to sound flippant. "Your grandad — he's such a hoarder. I ought to throw it all out."

"Gran." I reached out and put my hand on her arm. "I don't mean the boxes."

Gran looked down at my hand. She nodded, tightened her lips. Then I think she tried to say something, but it came out as a half-swallowed gulp, and a tear fell from her cheek onto my hand.

"It's Grandad, isn't it?" I asked.

She turned her tearstained face toward me and opened her mouth to speak. Then she shook her head. "I can't . . . It doesn't . . ." she began. Then she stopped and looked down again. She looked so lost and small, and suddenly I felt like the older one, the comforter. I wanted to protect her.

I put my other arm around her shoulders. For the first time in my life, I felt her relax into me.

"It's OK," I said. "You don't need to explain. I understand."

She looked back at me, a strange expression on her face. Shock. Disbelief. "You do?" she asked shakily.

"Of course I do. A family comes in, saying they've lost a member of *their* family. It's *bound* to upset you, with Grandad gone. It's set it all off again, made you scared in case he doesn't come back."

Then she half smiled and nodded. Pulling away from me, she reached out for my hand and gave it a squeeze. "You're right, dear," she said. "Of course that's what it is. I miss him so much. I just don't know what to do without him. Sometimes I think I'm going to go crazy if he doesn't come home. Sometimes I think I'm half-crazy already."

"He'll come home, Gran," I said. But I knew it was just words, and I couldn't hide my own uncertainty. "He will, won't he?" I added before I could stop myself.

Gran looked at me. "Of course he will," she said after a while. She smiled and stroked my face.

I smiled back, and as I met her eyes, I realized something. Whether or not either of us believed what we were saying didn't matter at that moment. What mattered was that we understood how much the other one needed to hear us say it.

"You're such a good girl, Amelia," Gran said softly.

Gran and I had never had a moment like this in our lives. It felt as if we'd finally found our way to the edge of the chasm that yawned between us and realized it wasn't that big. Right now, it felt as if it were so tiny we could have stepped across it all along.

The important thing was that we had done it now.

The other important thing—I suddenly remembered—was that there were people waiting for us downstairs.

"Come on," I said, reluctantly moving away from Gran. I stood up and reached a hand down to help her get up. "We need to get back to that family."

Gran looked at me and took my hand. "I'll just wash my face," she said. "You go down. Tell them I'll be there in a minute."

I nodded and turned to leave.

"Amelia," Gran said softly. I turned back. She smiled at me, and for the first time all week, the smile was genuine. It was a smile I'd never seen from Gran before. Open, warm, soft. "Thank you," she said simply.

I gave myself a moment to take in her words. I know they were quite simple and there were only two of them, but I couldn't remember the last time I'd heard her say them to me with so much feeling.

I smiled back at Gran. "You're welcome," I said. And as I headed downstairs a shiver of anxiety whipped through my body. I didn't know why I felt it, but something about the family waiting in the pub was making *me* uneasy, too.

By the time I took the drinks through to the lounge, Gran was behind me, and we went in together.

"I'm so sorry about that," Gran said breezily as soon as she came into the lounge. "I've been having a few dizzy spells recently. Think it's a bit of a bug. Now, let's see what we can do to help you. Where are you staying, first of all?"

Gran was all brisk business. It was as if she were a different person from the one who had been sobbing in my arms only moments earlier. She was back to being the one in charge, the one who looked after others, the one with no emotions.

"We're at Seaview Place," the man said. "But we have to be out this afternoon. We've been here a week."

"Our son didn't come back last night. We got in touch with the police first thing this morning, and they've got a team on it. They said they're sure he'll turn up today," his wife added, "but we'll obviously stay as long as it takes."

Gran glanced at Mom and me, nodded briskly, and said, "Well, you'll move in here for a few days."

The couple stared at Gran. So did Mom. The girl bit her lip and looked at her parents.

"I . . . I don't know if we . . ." the woman stammered.

Gran broke in. "No ifs," she said. "Most of our guests either checked out yesterday or they're leaving today. We've got plenty of rooms. You need to find your son."

"I think that's a great idea," the man said. "How much do —"

"And I don't want you paying," Gran said, before he even finished his question.

This time we *all* stared at her. "Your son has gone missing," Gran said firmly. "You need all the help and support you can find. You're staying here as our guests, and that's that."

Then she folded her arms and looked around at us all, challenging us to argue with her.

"Of course you must stay," Mom said, reaching out to touch the woman's arm. "We'll do everything we can to help you."

"You're very, very kind," the man said. He glanced at his wife and she gave a quick nod. "We'd love to stay here. Thank you."

The woman got her poster out of her bag again. "Before we go to get our things, could we put the poster up?"

"Of course you can," Gran said. "Amelia, fetch some tape and we'll put it in the window."

I ran to the kitchen and opened the junk drawer. Anything that didn't belong anywhere else usually ended up in there. Which meant it was always jam-packed with a hundred odd things you'd probably never need. I scrabbled through paper clips, lightbulbs, a folder full of kitchen appliance pamphlets, and finally found a roll of tape. I grabbed it and walked out.

I came back into the lounge and held the tape out to the woman.

"Why don't you just hang it up for them?" Gran said. "I'll show them their rooms."

The woman smiled at me. "Thank you so much," she said, almost in a whisper. Her eyes were brimming with tears she seemed determined to hold in.

I took the poster from her and was heading to the window with it when three things happened in quick succession that stopped me in my tracks.

The first thing was that the girl said, "I'll go back to the apartment and get Mitch."

The second thing was that Mom said, "Who's Mitch?" and the girl replied, "Our dog. He's a West Highland terrier."

The third thing was that I stopped breathing.

Mitch.

The piece of paper in my hands suddenly felt like it was on fire. I didn't want to hold it. And I certainly didn't want to look at it.

But I had to.

I could feel my heart thumping hard as I closed my eyes and turned the poster around.

I opened my eyes. Something that felt like a dagger made of ice sliced though my insides.

The boy in the photo on the poster was Peter.

Chapter Nine

I don't know how long I stared at his picture. All I knew was that I could hear everyone coming back downstairs and I was still standing next to the door, gaping at the poster they'd given me.

I shook myself and stuck it up in the window, and then I began asking myself questions I had no idea how to answer.

Like: what should I do? Should I tell them? Tell them what? That I'd met him? That I saw him yesterday? So what? It didn't mean anything. It might just make them think I had some answers, and I didn't want to give them false hope. The last thing I had was answers to any of this.

But what was the alternative? Say nothing?

"We'll be back later on, then," the woman was saying to Gran as they came back into the lounge. "We just need to take the rest of these posters around town — get them put up everywhere we can think of."

That was when I thought of an excuse to get out of the pub. If I did something useful, it might stop my brain buzzing with panicky half thoughts and unanswerable questions.

"I'll take them," I burst out. "You've got enough to do. You need to pack up and move in here and everything. Let me help."

The couple looked at me. "I can't believe you're all being so kind," the woman said. "You don't even know us, and you're all going out of your way like this — it's incredible."

I pretended to lace up my shoe so I could look down and hide my face. I didn't want any of them to see the guilty blush I could feel creeping around my neck and cheeks. Yes, I wanted to help. Of course I did. But I was doing this for me, too. I needed to do something about the disturbing thoughts that were beginning to knock at the outer edges of my mind. What if Peter *had* broken his promise? He had seemed like the kind of person who was true to his word — but what if he wasn't? What if he had taken the boat to Luffsands, after all? I had no idea how to find out, but maybe I could look for clues if I was out and about, rather than stuck here in the pub.

The man was looking at his daughter. "Why don't you go, too, hon? We can handle the packing."

For the first time, the girl glanced up and met my eyes. I wasn't sure I wanted her help. For the first time all week, I wasn't really hoping to make new friends. I wanted to be on my own to try to work things out in my head. But there was something about the way she gazed at me that made me think perhaps we could use each other's company. It was the expression in her eyes. She seemed lost, alone, and scared — pretty much how I was feeling at that moment. Plus, having someone else around would probably help to occupy my mind before my worries got out of control.

"That'd be great," I said.

The girl looked up at her parents and nodded. "OK."

Her mom exchanged a quick glance with her dad. "Don't go far," she said. "And stay together all the time, OK?"

"OK," we both replied. Then the girl took the rest of the posters from her mom and we set off into town.

"Hey, I don't even know your name," I said as we headed down the street toward the harbor front. I wrapped my arms around myself as we walked. I'd been in such a hurry to get out that I'd forgotten to grab a coat. Still, it was mild out and it wasn't raining, so I didn't suggest going back for it. I couldn't face returning to the pub just yet.

"Sal," she said. "What's yours?"

"Mia," I said. "Well, my real name's Amelia, but no one calls me that anymore, except my gran — or my parents if they're yelling at me about something!"

I smiled, and Sal smiled back. "I know what you mean," she said. "Everyone calls me Sal. My middle name's Elizabeth, and very occasionally, my parents call me Sally Elizabeth. It doesn't happen very often, but I *know* I'm in trouble when it does!"

I laughed, and suddenly I felt lighter than I'd felt in hours. There was something about Sal that felt easy and nice. She was probably about my age, and she probably had about as many people to talk to around here as I did. If it weren't for the fact that we were looking for her missing brother, we could probably have had a good time together.

"Do you and Peter get along well?" I asked as we turned the corner onto the seafront.

Sal shrugged. "OK, I guess. We don't argue, if that's what you mean."

"I can't imagine Peter arguing with anyone," I said before I could stop myself.

Sal suddenly stopped walking and looked at me. "What do you mean? You know my brother?"

My cheeks heated up as though I'd been caught in a lie. But I hadn't. I hadn't done anything wrong. I had nothing to hide.

"Yeah, I've met him on the beach a couple of times," I mumbled.

I held my breath as Sal continued to stare at me. Then she turned away and continued walking. "Well, you're right," she said. "That is the kind of person he is. He gets along with everyone."

I let my breath out and fell into step beside her.

"I just hope nothing's happened to him. I couldn't bear it if he . . . I just want him back," she said.

"We'll get him back," I said firmly. "We'll find him."

We walked in silence after that. I kept trying to

think of something else I could say to make her feel better, but I had nothing. Part of me wanted to tell her about what we'd nearly done — how Peter had wanted to take the boat out — but what was the point? I already had it in *my* mind, getting all tangled up in my thoughts, hopes, fears. She didn't need it doing the same thing to her.

And anyway, Peter had sworn he wouldn't take the boat out. He'd *promised*. Telling Sal a half story about something that almost definitely hadn't even happened wouldn't help.

There was only one option: we *had* to find him.

"Look. Should we take a poster in there?" Sal was pointing to a shop at the far end of the harbor, a boating store called Shipshape.

"Good idea. We should try everywhere. We can ask if they've seen him as well."

We hurried toward the shop.

A bell clanged halfheartedly as we pushed open the door.

"Hello?" I called. There was no one around.

I'd never been in the shop before. I must have walked past it a hundred times and hardly noticed it. Boat fenders and ropes and fishhooks had never been my thing, so it was hardly surprising. But now that we were inside, I wished I'd taken a look sooner.

"It's like a whole other world in here," Sal whispered, echoing my thoughts.

Rows and rows of shelves ran the length of the shop, each one crammed with every item you would ever need if you were planning a trip out to sea.

Ropes coiled into circles so big they were like mini rotaries; anchors in every size, from something that looked like a pair of garden shears to one that must have been twice my height; charts that looked as if they could have helped you plot your way to the moon; a gazillion fishing rods. All of them stacked and stuffed into every available bit of space in the shop.

"Hello?" I called again as we tiptoed along a row of bright-yellow raincoats toward the counter in the far corner of the shop.

Sal pointed to a brass bell on the counter. "Shall we . . . ?"

"I guess so."

Sal picked up the bell and shook it. It echoed around the shop. No one came. I was about to suggest we give up, when I heard a shuffling sound from a room behind the counter.

An elderly man appeared in the doorway. His hair — what there was of it — was wild and wispy, as if he'd just gotten out of bed. He had a shiny bald patch in the middle of his head, and as he stood there, he flattened a few strands of hair across it from one side.

His face was pocked with scars, as though they had a lifetime's stories of battles to tell.

He turned a pair of piercing green eyes toward us and squinted. "Can I help you?" he asked gruffly.

Sal took a step forward. "We, um, we wondered if we could put this up." She peeled off one of the posters and held it out to the man. "It's my brother," she explained as the man pulled a pair of glasses out of his pocket, wiped them with the corner of his shirt, and slipped them on. "He's missing," she added.

The old man took the poster and scanned it silently for a few moments. Then he looked up slowly and turned his gaze on both of us. Something that might have been a smile flickered across his eyes. *Was he laughing at us?*

"It's not a joke," I said quickly. "It's really serious. He's gone, and we need to find him."

The man put the poster down on his desk. The smile still seemed to be there, glinting deep inside his strange green eyes. Then he shook his head. "I'm not laughing," he said carefully. Then he turned his back on us.

Sal and I exchanged a glance. "So you'll put our poster up?" Sal asked.

The man waved a hand at us without turning back around. "Aye, I'll put your poster up."

And with that, he shuffled off into the back room he'd come from.

Was that it?

"Do you think he's coming back?" Sal whispered.

"I don't know. Should we just hang on a minute and see?" I whispered back.

We waited for a minute. Then another. Finally, I turned to Sal. "I think we should go," I said. "He said he'll put it up."

"We could pop back later, just to see if it's in the window," she suggested.

"Good idea. Come on, let's go."

We turned and made our way back through the shop. Sal opened the front door and we were about to leave when the man called from the back of the shop.

"So, which one of you is Mia?" he asked.

We stopped in our tracks so quickly that if we'd been playing freeze dance, we'd have tied for first place.

I was the first to recover. I turned toward the man. *"I'm* Mia," I said shakily.

The man nodded. "Thought so. Just checking," he said. Then he held out a plastic bag and added, "This is for you."

I stared at him from across the shop. Then, feeling like a doll made of wood, I somehow walked back to the counter and stood in front of him. Sal followed me.

The man put the bag down on the counter. As I glanced at it, my stomach seemed to coil up inside me as tightly as the fishing ropes at my feet.

The bag had my name on it.

The man shoved it across to me. "For Mia" was scribbled on the side in a faded marker pen. As I stood staring down at it, he reached under the counter for a pouch of tobacco and some cigarette papers. "Are you going to take it then?" he asked, pulling off a paper and spreading tobacco across it.

"Is it really for me?" I asked. "I mean, how do you know I'm the right Mia? How did you even know I was Mia at all? Who left it for me?"

The man rolled his cigarette and lit it. Then he exhaled a line of smoke and coughed a long, rasping cough. When he'd finished, he wiped his hand across his head again and said, "Which of those questions would you like me to answer first, my dear?"

"How did you know I was Mia?" I asked.

"Gave me a description," the man said.

"Who did?" Sal asked.

"Boy who left the bag." The man shrugged. "Said his name was Peter."

"Peter?" Sal gasped. *"Peter?"*

My stomach twisted into another knot. Peter had been here! He'd left something for me! What was it? And when had he left it? Since I last saw him? *Since he'd disappeared?*

And why had he come in here, anyway?

The old man pointed at the poster. "Plus, he looked like that. Same scruffy hairdo, anyway."

"When did he come in?" Sal asked, her voice coming out in a kind of tight squeak.

"Oh, a little while ago. He said I might be waiting some time for you." The man took another long suck on his cigarette. "He was right about that," he added, and suddenly burst out laughing.

His laughter soon turned into a wheezing, rasping cough. As he was laughing and coughing, a phone on his desk started ringing. The man picked it up, turning his back on us as if we weren't there.

"Eric Travers," he said curtly into the phone.

I walked around to the other side of the counter and stared at him until he looked at me.

"When did he leave it?" I whispered.

He waved a hand at me as if to shoo me away.

"It's important," I said.

He frowned at me. "Just hold on a second, will you?" he said into the phone. Then he cupped a hand over the mouthpiece and turned to both of us. "I'm done. Go on with you, now," he said roughly.

"But—"

"But nothing. Go. I've given you the package. I've done my bit. I don't want any more to do with this."

"Please, Mr. Travers," Sal began. "It's really imp—"

"I said GO!"

Sal and I looked at each other. She raised her eyebrows in a question. I shrugged back a reply, and we turned and began to scurry out before the weird old man shouted at us again.

"Hey!" he shouted at us when we were halfway down one of the aisles.

I turned back around. He was holding the plastic bag in his hand. "Don't forget your package."

I ran back and grabbed the bag. I'd been so freaked out by everything I'd almost forgotten it.

"Thanks," I said. Then I turned and hurried out of the door, while the man went back to his phone call.

Sal was outside sitting on a bench overlooking the harbor.

"Well, that was weird," I said, plunking myself down next to her.

"Just a bit," Sal replied.

I turned to face her. "You want to go back and tell your parents?" I asked.

She shook her head. "I want to get the rest of these posters up first — and find out what's in that package."

"OK," I agreed. "But when we get back, whatever else we do, we're calling the police," I said firmly.

Sal swallowed. "What are we going to tell them?"

I took a breath and turned away as I slowly let it out again. "That we might have just met the last person to have seen Peter before he disappeared."

Diane

She sat by the window all day. Well, perhaps not the entire day. The first hour after her father had left was spent in her bedroom, shouting, cursing, pacing her room so hard it was a wonder there was any carpet left when she finally stopped.

Finally, she tore a page out of one of her mother's notebooks, and began to write her feelings down. It was the only way she could get them out. She would have used her diary but she had sent that away with her father.

She wrote about how angry she was with her father, how he spoiled everything, how she hated him, hated Luffsands, hated everything right now.

Finally, when the anger was out, she wrote about her fear.

Eventually, all she wrote was, "Father, please come home soon. I love you and I just want you to be safe. I'm sorry. I'll never get angry with you again, I promise. Just come home, please."

After that, she put down her pen, folded up the paper, and went downstairs. When she had hugged her mother tightly and whispered an apology that she wished her father would hear, she took herself to the window seat and sat, looking out at the sea raging below and trying to calm her heart.

It was still two hours before high tide and already the angry swell was rising fiercely, beating against the harbor wall like an angry mob that would not recede until it had wreaked the havoc it craved. The few boats inside the small harbor reared like rodeo horses with every wave. Each time, Diane's heart reared with them, so hard she feared it would come out through her mouth if she wasn't careful.

She watched the sea level inching ever higher with the tide, watched the swell grow more and more angry, all the time desperately hoping to see her father's boat returning.

Why had she let him leave her in such a mood? She faced directly out the window and offered her plea bargain to the sea: bring my father home, just let him come home today, and I swear I'll never say a mean word to him again.

Finally, with nothing left to barter, and all out of wishes, she curled up in the seat, closed her eyes, and prayed.

Chapter Ten

"Are you going to open it, then?"

Sal was perched on the bench next to me. The package was on my lap. I didn't know exactly how long we'd both been sitting staring at it, and I didn't really know what Sal made of what had just happened. I didn't know what *I* made of it. My brain turned over and over, trying to find an angle that made sense. Here's what I had come up with. It wasn't much.

I'd seen Peter yesterday. He'd wanted to take the boat out but he'd promised he wouldn't. At some point after that, he'd gone missing.

That was about it. And in among the thin scraps of information that wouldn't piece together was one question that nagged at my mind: *did he take the boat?*

I looked at Sal. Her eyes were full of sadness and confusion. I couldn't keep the doubts to myself any longer.

"Sal," I began. "I need to tell you something."

She looked up. "What?"

I opened my mouth to continue, but I couldn't find the words. Surely my doubts would only make her even more anxious. And was it fair to give her even more to worry about?

No, I couldn't do it. I couldn't give her an extra burden to carry, as well as what she was already feeling.

And another thing, if Peter had delivered this bag to the shop, didn't that mean that he was still on the mainland?

Truth was, there were still too many question marks surrounding my troubled thoughts, and it simply wasn't fair to share them with Sal till I knew where they would lead. Which meant I had to come up with some way of finding out where that might be. Or coming up with a plan, at least.

I smiled at her. "I just want to say, I'm sure it'll all work out," I said. "We'll find him."

Sal smiled back. "Thanks," she said. "I really think we will, now that we've got you and your family helping. The police were helpful, but I could tell they thought Peter was just a typical teenage boy — going off without telling anyone — and he'd turn up any minute. At least I feel like we're doing something useful now. Your family has been so kind."

I wasn't sure she really had anything to thank me for. If my looming worries turned out to be right, it could well be that *I* was the reason Peter had disappeared in the first place.

It was time to change the subject.

"OK, let's take a look at this package," I said. I pulled at the tape and opened the bag.

"What is it?" Sal asked as I lifted out the object that was inside — a big round brass dome. I turned it over in my hands.

"Wait, look — it opens up," I said. There was a catch on the top of the dome. I clicked the catch and slid it open. The top half slid underneath and clicked into place, to leave a semicircular dome shape with a flat glass surface on top. Inside the glass was a large star surrounded by a bunch of letters and numbers, and with a dial in the middle.

"A compass," Sal said. "I don't understand."

"Neither do I," I said. I stared at the compass. There was something familiar about it. Had we used something like this in school? Did Dad have one at home? Or maybe there was one at the pub. That was probably it. It was exactly the kind of thing Grandad would have in the lounge somewhere!

Sal pointed at the bag. "There's something else in it," she said.

I rummaged in the bag and pulled out a folded piece of paper. I opened it up.

We both leaned over it, trying to figure out what we were looking at. At first glance, I'd have said it was a piece of trash that had accidentally gotten into the bag with the compass. It was crumpled and ragged and looked like the kind of thing you'd find down the back of a very old sofa.

Someone had doodled all over the page. Words I couldn't read, as they were heavily crossed out. Scribbled pictures of arrows pointing in every direction, most of these crossed out, too. The only ones that weren't were the ones pointing directly upward.

In the top-right corner, a capital "N" stood out. It was the only letter on the page that wasn't crossed out.

"Just a piece of trash," Sal said. "Must have gotten in by mistake."

I was about to throw it away in a nearby waste-basket, but just as I was scrunching it up, I noticed writing on the other side. I opened up the paper again and turned it over.

Keep this compass with the boat!!!!!

The message was written in thick black pen and underlined so heavily there was a small rip where the pen had gone through the paper. I read it out loud.

"What does that mean?" Sal asked. "What boat?"

I shook my head. "No idea."

Then she looked at the note over my shoulder, and she turned whiter than the paper itself.

"Are you OK?" I asked.

She nodded, and then, pointing at the words, she said something that made my blood turn so cold I almost felt ice cubes forming in my chest.

"It's Peter's writing," she said. "Whatever this means, it's a message for us — and it's *definitely* from him."

Her voice cracked as she spoke. Which was when I knew I had to tell her everything. It didn't matter if it led to despair or doubts. What mattered now was that we were in this together.

"Sal," I said softly.

She looked up.

"Just, I . . . well, I . . ." I looked away from her. "Look, there's something I need to tell you," I said as I looked out at the beach, the water rolling and frothing around the harbor wall. Where should I start?

"About Peter?" Sal asked.

I nodded.

"Did he . . . Are you and he, you know . . ."

"No!" I burst out. "It's nothing like that! I've only met him twice, and most of the time we just talked about the dogs."

Sal laughed lightly. "That doesn't surprise me. Peter loves Mitch."

"Yeah, I could tell."

"What is it, then? What do you want to tell me?"

"Well, like I said, Peter was really friendly. And helpful. And he wanted to try to cheer me up. You see, I've got a kind of friend. She lives on an island just off the coast, and she was supposed to come here yesterday, but she couldn't make it."

"So, what has that got to do with Peter?" Sal's voice was starting to get an edge of impatience.

"He wanted to help me. He wanted us to go and fetch her."

"Fetch her? How?"

"On a boat," I said shakily. "He wanted us to take a boat."

"What? Peter steal a boat? No way — he'd never do that. That's not him at all."

"No, he didn't want to steal it. It was Dee's boat."

"Dee?"

"My friend. It was her dad's boat. Peter suggested that we could borrow it to go and get her. We were on our way out of the harbor when my mom turned up and called me back."

Sal was staring at me. "How come you haven't told me any of this before now?" she asked.

"Because he promised he wouldn't go on his own. He *swore* he wouldn't. It was one thing for me to borrow the boat, but for Peter to take it when none of the family would have known who he was — well, it would have been hard to explain without it looking like theft."

Sal was quiet for a long time. She looked at me, slowly nodded her head. "You're right," she said firmly. "And Peter is no thief."

"I know he isn't," I said. "That's why I didn't say —"

"But the thing he likes to do most in the world is help people," Sal continued, her face clouding over as she spoke. We sat in silence, both of us staring blankly ahead.

Then Sal turned back to me. She was trying to say something.

"What? What are you thinking?" I asked.

She shook her head. "I'm trying to figure out which would have been the stronger pull for Peter. The desire to help you, or the knowledge that he shouldn't take someone else's boat."

"And?"

"And they feel neck and neck right now."

I nodded.

"And you didn't see him again after this?"

I shook my head.

"So what we're saying is that Peter might have gone out on some boat, on his own, and that was the last anyone saw of him," Sal said woodenly.

"I'm sorry. I should have told you before. I should have told *everyone*—"

"No, you shouldn't have," Sal stopped me. "If Mom even *suspected* this, it could tip her over the edge. You were right to wait till you were sure."

"But I'm not," I said. "I'm not sure at all. If anything, I'm more confused than ever."

Sal smiled shyly. "Yeah, but at least we can be confused together now."

I smiled back. "Thank you," I said quietly.

"Anyway, if he left you this package, doesn't that mean he *didn't* go out on the boat?" Sal asked. "Or, if he did, that he made it back here safely?"

"That's exactly what I thought. But if he's on the mainland, why didn't he go back to you and your parents last night?"

Sal shook her head. "I've no idea. But if he left on the boat and didn't come back, when could he have taken the package to the shop for you?"

I let out a breath. I didn't have any answers. Every time I thought I had one, it only led to more questions. I turned the compass around and around in my hands, looking at it and thinking so hard my brain was beginning to hurt. And then, finally, a plan came to me.

"Sal," I said, staring at the compass.

"What?" Sal asked.

I held the compass out to her, pointing at a lever at the bottom of the dome where you hooked it into place on a matching part. A matching part that we didn't have here. A matching part that I now knew I had definitely seen before — and not at the pub.

I shivered as I spoke. "I know where I've seen this before," I said. "It's the compass from Dee's dad's boat. And it was *definitely* on the boat when I last saw it. We just need to find the boat and then, hopefully, we'll find the first clue to what's happened to Peter."

We walked along the coast path, heading back toward town and the beach and the old jetty where the boat was usually moored. Maybe it was there. If it was, surely we'd be on the way to solving this puzzle, wouldn't we?

Sal was first to break the silence. "Do you think we should go back to the pub and tell our families everything first?" she asked hesitantly.

"Do you want to?"

"Do *you*?" She held my eyes.

How should I answer? With what I wanted to do, or what I thought we *should* do? Truth was, I couldn't say for sure I knew what was the right thing to do for anyone anymore. I decided to go with my gut feeling.

"No, not yet. Not till we can offer them something more than a hundred bits of information that don't add up."

She breathed out. "I agree."

"OK, good," I said, scanning the coastline below

us as we walked. "Come on, let's just see if the boat is at the—"

I stopped talking *and* walking. Something had caught my eye in the cove directly below us.

"What's up?" Sal asked. "Why've you stopped?"

I stared down into the cove so hard my eyes began to water. There was something bobbing down there. A boat. It wasn't tied to anything, but was drifting in and out with the waves, almost beached but still just afloat.

As I stared down at it, I became more and more positive that it wasn't just any boat. It was *the* boat! My throat clogged up and tingles pricked at my scalp.

I held a shaky hand out to point to it.

"That's — that's it!" I gasped.

Sal stopped walking and followed the line of my hand. "That's what?"

"Dee's dad's boat! The one Peter wanted to go out on! The one I was heading to the harbor to see if we could find. It looks like it's been washed up in that bay."

Sal turned to me. "You're kidding!"

I squinted and stared hard at the boat. It was the same shape; it had a wheelhouse in the center that looked identical; it was the same color. But then, how many boats in the harbor were more or less identical to this one?

"I . . . I don't know," I said, suddenly losing my confidence. "I can't be sure."

"But it could be?"

I chewed at the inside of my cheek. "Yes," I said finally. "It definitely could be." Then, without giving it any more thought, I left the coast path and headed for the path that led down to the bay.

"What are you doing?" Sal asked, half running to keep up with me.

"Going to check it out," I answered without slowing my stride.

We reached the edge of the promontory and looked down at the stony path — what there was of it. It looked as if there'd been multiple landslides that had eroded the path. Stones were scattered all around and the ground looked rough and slippery — and so steep it was almost vertical.

Sal looked down. "Do you think it's safe?"

It looked a *long* way from safe. But what other options did we have? If that was Dee's dad's boat, we might only have minutes to get to it before it was washed back out to sea again.

"I'll go first," I said. "Just follow me and take every step carefully. We'll be fine."

Sal nodded and chewed on a fingernail. "I'm not

great with heights at the best of times," she said, her voice a pitch higher than usual and her breath short and raspy in between her words.

"I know. Me neither — but your brother could be down there!" I said. "This is our best chance of finding Peter, or at least finding a clue to what's happened to him."

Sal stopped chewing her nail. "You're right," she said firmly. "Come on, then."

We lowered ourselves carefully onto the start of the path.

"Mia."

I turned back to Sal. "Yes?"

"What if . . . What if we climb all the way down there and find it's a different boat?"

I held her eyes. "We'll deal with that when we get there," I said. "But there's only one way to find out."

She nodded and gave me a tiny smile. "OK," she said. "Let's go."

After that, we didn't say another word as we picked our way carefully down the steep, gravelly path to the deserted cove below.

"It's the one, I'm sure of it," I said as we waded up to our knees to get to the boat. We'd taken off our shoes and rolled up our jeans. Holding my shoes in one hand, I ignored the freezing cold of the water as I examined the boat. "It's *identical*."

"You're positive?" Sal asked, standing shivering beside me. "You did say they all look the same."

"No. Look at this." I pointed to the back of the boat. "See those two black lines? Dee's dad's boat has those."

"But wouldn't any boat have something like that if it's kept alongside a jetty? From rubbing against it?"

She was right. I couldn't honestly say I was absolutely positive. And, in fact, as well as the black lines from rubbing against a jetty, this one seemed to have far more marks and gashes and scratches than I'd remembered. Its registration number did begin "PN" like Dee's dad's — but I couldn't remember the rest of the number.

"Peter isn't on board, anyway," Sal said flatly. "Although, at least that's better than finding him here and discovering he's —"

"No." I stopped her. "Don't say it. Don't say anything like it." I tried to pull myself up so I could get onto the boat. From this angle, it was proving difficult, especially as it kept on swaying against me and then away again with the waves.

"Look, give me a leg up," I said. "Let's get on board."

I bent my knee and Sal heaved me up till I could clamber over the side. Then I reached down to help her up. We dried our legs with a couple of rags and put our shoes back on.

"Do you see anything that confirms it either way?" Sal asked as we stood on the deck, holding on to the wheelhouse to keep steady while we examined the boat.

Mostly what I saw was mess everywhere. The boat was full of seaweed and stones, and the deck and benches were wet. The ropes were strewn around in a sandy, tangled mess, and the cabin door was swinging open, with crab pots lying on their sides in front of it.

"Well, it's got crab pots," I said. "Dee's dad had them." Then I thought of something else, something that would tell me for sure. I carefully made my way to the back of the boat. The back locker had a pile of ropes and seaweed in front of it. I moved them out of the way and opened the locker.

Dee's diary was there!

I pulled out the book and held it up, beaming as though it were a gold medal.

"What's that?" Sal asked.

"Dee's diary! Now I'm *positive.* A hundred percent. This is *definitely* the right boat."

I sat down and flipped through the pages to see if

there was anything new that could help us figure out what had happened. But the last entry was the one I'd read yesterday—which meant Dee almost certainly hadn't gotten her diary back, so the boat probably hadn't gotten to her. And *that* meant . . . that meant . . . what? That Peter hadn't taken the boat, or that he'd taken it but never reached Luffsands?

"Something terrible has happened to Peter, hasn't it?" Sal said, echoing the dark fear that was creeping through my body, prickling the hairs along my arms and scratching at my neck.

I wanted to tell her she was wrong. I wanted to reassure her, but I couldn't. "I don't know," I said eventually, as I shoved the diary into my bag. I didn't want to leave it in the locker. I wanted to keep it near me. I knew it was stupid, but it made me feel as if we were closer to finding Peter if I had Dee's words nearby.

Sal nodded. Then she started making her way around the boat, straightening the ropes into slightly neater coils, lifting the lids on the benches.

"What are you doing?" I asked.

"I'm looking for anything that might tell us if Peter was here. Maybe he left a clue behind. He might have even written us a note or something."

In my heart, I didn't really think we'd find anything.

If he was going to leave us a note on the boat, why would he have gone to the bother of leaving the package at the shop? But it was better than doing nothing, so we searched the boat together.

Then I had another thought. I lifted the back bench seat.

At first, all I could see was a couple of buckets full of fishing hooks and bait and tools, and a crumpled-up fisherman's coat like the one Peter had just bought, only older and grubbier. I searched through it all, looking for the key.

It wasn't there.

I decided not to tell Sal. After all, it didn't mean anything. Peter could have taken the key with him when he left — if he'd been here at all. Then I had another thought: the wheelhouse.

I went inside, and my heart leaped as though it had a flying fish inside it.

The key was in the ignition.

Sal was behind me. She stopped in the doorway. "What is it?" she asked.

"The key . . ." I didn't know what else to say.

Sal looked where I was pointing. "It's still here," she said. "What does that mean?"

"I don't know," I replied, trying to keep my voice

calm and soothing. "But, look, it doesn't necessarily mean anything bad. We still don't know Peter took the boat out."

Sal had turned away. Suddenly, she pushed the door closed and reached down to pick up something that had gotten trapped behind it. She looked at me, her face as white as the waves spraying onto the beach. She was holding something I'd seen only yesterday.

A coat. Similar to the one I'd just seen in the bench seat — only this one was brand-new. It was Peter's coat. And he had *definitely* been wearing it when I last saw him.

"I think," Sal said, "that perhaps, now, we do."

I swallowed. "He'll be OK," I said. "I'm sure there'd be something more obvious if he . . . if he . . ."

"Don't say it," Sal said.

She was right. We couldn't even entertain the thought that Peter had met with some kind of accident out at sea. However likely or possible it might be, it simply wasn't something we could think about right now.

"OK, look, let's think positively," I said. "As long as we assume nothing terrible has happened to Peter, I reckon there are two options. Either he came back to the mainland on the boat . . ."

Sal shook her head. "If he'd done that, he'd have

come back to see us. I'm *sure* he would. There's no way he'd have left us worrying if he was nearby. What's the other option?"

"That he got to Luffsands and got off there. And somehow he lost the boat. Maybe he didn't tie it up properly, and he got stuck over there." I thought for a moment. "And I guess there's a third possibility as well," I added.

"What's that?"

"That he never took the boat out after all. Only, that would have to mean that he tied the boat up and then, for some reason, took off his coat and left it on board before getting off."

"Why would he do that?" Sal asked. "It doesn't make sense."

No, it doesn't, I thought. *None* of this made sense.

"OK, then," Sal said. She nodded slowly, as if making a deal with herself. Then, her jaw set firm, she came to stand by my side. She gave me a tiny look, and even though she didn't say anything, I knew what she was thinking.

I moved to one side. Sal took my place at the wheel.

As she steadied herself and looked at all the dials in front of her, I took the compass out of the bag and reached over to the stand above the steering wheel.

The stand was loose, as though the compass had been pulled out of it too roughly. I tightened a screw on its side and then very carefully placed the compass inside it. It clicked firmly into place as though it belonged there.

Which was, of course, because it did.

Sal turned to me and raised her eyebrows. Still without a single word passing between us, I nodded. She nodded back. Then she turned the key. The engine sputtered to life.

Part of me was screaming, *What on earth are we doing?*

Another part of me — the stronger part, and the part I was listening to — knew exactly what we were doing.

We were going to find Peter.

Chapter Eleven

Sal heaved the wheel around so the boat was facing out to sea.

"You do know how to drive it, don't you?" I asked as we motored out of the bay, heading toward Luffsands.

Sal replied without turning around. "*I* did the course too, you know. Peter might have been the one to get all the praise from the fishermen, but I think that's only because he's a boy. While they were all telling him how clever he was, and showing him how to prepare a line for catching mackerel, I drove the boat just as much," she said. "And just as well!"

Yes, and for all we know, Peter drove the boat into life-threatening danger.

I was glad Sal was facing away from me. I didn't want her to see my face and guess what I was thinking.

"I trust you," I said. And I meant it. I had no choice. This was the best plan we'd come up with so far. Well, it was the *only* plan. I had to believe Peter would be at Luffsands, and I had to believe Sal would get us there safely. As I glanced back at the coastline — already quite a distance away — I knew there was no option B.

"Can you imagine their faces if we turn up at the pub with Peter?" Sal asked as she drove.

"If?" I replied, mainly to show her I'd meant what I'd said about putting my trust in her. "Don't you mean *when*?"

Sal briefly turned around to grin at me. I found myself relaxing a little and smiling back. Anyway, she was right. How awesome would it be to go back to our families, not just saying we'd put a few posters up but that we'd found Peter and brought him home!

"OK, which direction is Luffsands?" Sal asked.

I thought back to Dee's letters. "North."

Sal consulted the compass and gently turned the wheel this way and that, correcting the direction as she went, and taking us farther and farther out to sea on water that was so still and clear I could see the bottom, even when we were a long way out from the cove.

I began to relax. If it hadn't been for the reason we were doing this in the first place, I might even have enjoyed it.

I looked around us while Sal drove. I don't know what I was looking for, exactly. It's not as if I was expecting to see Peter out here in the ocean waving to us to bring him home. The thought made me shudder.

After a little while, the island was clearly in view. The side we were coming in on was covered in trees, still bare from a long winter.

"We have to go around the island," I said. "The village is on the other side."

Sal turned the boat.

As we rounded the side of the island, I glanced at the compass. The arrow was pointing exactly north. At that moment, a breeze caught the boat from the back, making it lurch so that I slipped and fell against Sal.

"Whoops, sorry," I said. Just then, the wind caught us again. This time, we both fell.

"Wow, it's getting windy," Sal said. "Do you think we should —"

She didn't get to finish her question, as the boat suddenly lurched sideways. A massive wave had come from nowhere and hit us sideways, bucketing water onto the deck. I crashed against the wheelhouse door, nearly falling out onto the deck myself, as the boat dipped sharply backward. Another wave was rearing up toward us. It was heading straight for the side of the boat. What was going on?

The sea had been as calm as a pond a second ago. Suddenly, it was a raging torrent of mountainous waves. The sky had blackened and rain was now lashing down so hard it was almost impossible to see. The window was streaked with rain and was beginning to steam up.

"What's happening?" Sal screamed over the sound of the rain and waves.

"I don't know!" I cried, grabbing on to the wheel with her, to help her steer us around so that the next wave didn't hit us from the side, too. They seemed to be coming from every angle, but the ones hitting us sideways were the worst. "Freak storm? Maybe it'll pass in a minute."

I glanced at the compass to get some bearings, and I saw the strangest thing. The arrow was spinning around and around, pointing every which way.

"Sal — the compass."

Sal looked at it. "What's it doing?" she gasped over the thunderous waves.

"I don't know. Just keep heading in the same direction, and hopefully we'll get around to Luffsands soon."

"Maybe if we can get closer in, the sea will be calmer," Sal said. "I need to change course. Hold on."

I held on while Sal swung the boat to the left so we approached the waves at an angle that felt safer. The boat stopped veering so violently from side to side, and I stopped thinking we were going to capsize at any moment. We climbed up waves that were twice the size of our boat, and slid down the other side, holding our breath each time — but at least we had stopped plunging around like a rodeo horse.

The rain seemed to have eased off too, and I went back outside to wipe the window down and look around.

"Sal, look!" I called, pointing over to the left. "Luffsands! We're almost there!" We were approaching the village from the eastern side. "We have to reach the harbor."

The only problem with that was it meant we had to go sideways to the waves again, and they were even worse now that we were around on this side of the island — the side that was open to the ocean rather than facing the mainland. I held tight as the boat climbed and plunged and rocked, water spraying over the sides like a waterfall with every wave.

"Here!" Sal called to me. She was holding out Peter's coat. "Put it on. You're getting soaked."

I grabbed the coat from her. It was at least two sizes too big for me, but I didn't care. We weren't exactly at a fashion show. I put it on.

Eventually, the harbor came into view again. Or, to be more precise, it came and went, rising and falling with the waves. Every now and then, the island disappeared from sight completely as the swell continued to beat its way toward the harbor, lifting us high, then dumping us down into dark, watery wells.

Tight-lipped, Sal managed to steer us toward the harbor. But that was when we realized — there *was* no harbor! Or at least, not one that we stood much chance of getting into.

The outer wall was just about there, but once we got close, we could see that the water had risen so high there were no jetties to aim for. Even the harbor wall itself was much lower than the one in Porthaven — it had sunk beneath the rising water!

"What are we going to do?" I asked. "How can we get the boat near enough to shore to get off it?"

Sal was scanning the harbor, as I was. There was

absolutely nothing high enough above the waterline for us to tie up to. I didn't like our chances, anyway. The waves were so vicious they would have thrown us against what there was of the wall and broken the boat up.

Sal shook her head. "We can get into the harbor, but there's no way we'll be able to tie up — not without getting smashed to smithereens."

"I know," I said, all the hope I'd felt earlier draining out of me. It drained even quicker a moment later, when the rain eased enough for me to see beyond the harbor itself and into the village.

"Sal," I said hoarsely. "Look."

The sea wall at the bottom of the village had been completely destroyed. Chunks of bricks and broken pieces of rock lay scattered in the water. The sea had dug massive craters in the sand below.

The front row of houses had all but collapsed. There were seven of them, but they had all lost their roofs. Two had gaping holes instead of windows and sloped at an angle, as though trying hard not to slip completely into the sea, but knowing they were about to fail. The other five, which were slightly farther forward than the rest, were only visible from the second floor upward. Their ground floors were totally submerged.

I tried to calm my breathing. Had all this damage only just happened? How could that be possible? The storm had only just begun. Surely it hadn't had enough time to wreak destruction like this?

Dee's house. Where was it? I tried to remember if she'd told me where it was.

Sal edged the boat closer and closer to the shore. Now that we were inside the harbor wall, the sea was calmer. We still rose and fell with the swell, but the waves weren't beating against us or hurling us down into dark canyons anymore.

I scanned the houses, looking for anything familiar from Dee's descriptions. Looking for any signs of life.

And then I saw a group of houses that I recognized from Dee's diary; a group of three that stood on a piece of ground slightly higher than the front row. They were nearby, but given our chances of getting to them, they might as well have been a mile away.

All three houses were standing in water that reached to their second floors, and all the top windows had been blown out. The first two houses had no roofs. The third still had a partial roof.

Wait! There was someone on that roof — waving and calling!

I rubbed the salty spray out of my eyes and realized that it wasn't just one person, it was two.

And one of them was Peter.

I could see a long jetty jutting out from the northern end of the seafront. The only trouble was, it was almost completely submerged. Every now and then, as a wave subsided, we could just see a pole sticking out of the waves, but it wasn't tall enough to tie up to without running the risk of the boat being dragged underwater by the swell.

We couldn't pull up to the beach, either — or what had presumably been a beach at some point, anyway. The whole of the front of the village was rubble and rocks, with more falling from the front row of houses all the time. It was too dangerous to attempt it.

There was simply no way in.

"How are we going to get to them?" Sal asked, panicked.

"I don't know!" I was searching all along the shore, but could see nothing that would help us. Waving my arms in the air to let them know we'd seen them, I kept my eyes on Peter and the girl with him, who must have been Dee.

They waved back.

"Sal, we've got to rescue them," I said hoarsely.

"I know."

Sal brought us as near to the harbor wall as she could, edging closer to the shore a tiny bit at a time, creeping in on the swell but keeping a safe enough distance out that the waves couldn't hurl us against the wall. She held our position as carefully as she could. She had been right. She *was* excellent at driving the boat.

"This is the best I'm going to manage," she said when we were still quite a way from the sunken jetty. "It's just not safe to go any farther in."

I waved across at Peter. Then I cupped my mouth with my hands and shouted as loudly as I could, "Can you get down?"

Peter shook his head.

"They heard me!" I called to Sal. She gave me a thumbs-up sign while she continued to grip the wheel and keep us away from the rocky edge of the island.

"Can't leave roof!" Peter called. "Beams collapsed on top floor. Ground floor totally flooded."

"How did you get up there?" I called.

"Chimney!"

They'd climbed up through the chimney?

"I got thrown from the boat by massive wave. Tried to get back on board, but the boat disappeared. Thought it had sunk!"

"We found the boat!" I yelled, kicking myself for stating the obvious — we'd *obviously* found it. We were *on* it! "Are you OK?" I called.

"Kind of. We were trapped inside for hours. I think the rescue workers have come — everyone else seems to be gone!"

Rescue workers? If they'd been here, how come we hadn't heard anything about it?

"Mia, help us!" Peter shouted. He sounded so desperate — it broke my heart, and strengthened it at the same time. We *had* to get them out of there.

"We'll save you!" I called back. "Just hang on."

"Dee's mom — she's inside! Trapped under a beam. We can't get her out."

I stared at Peter, trying to comprehend how Dee must be feeling. She hadn't even spoken yet. She was gripping the roof of her home with both hands, barely even looking our way, her face as white as the foam from the breaking waves all around us.

"Be quick! Please!" Peter yelled.

I swallowed hard. I didn't know what to say. "We'll get you all out," I managed eventually.

I was about to turn away when I remembered something. The note — the one he'd presumably left for us.

"We got the package."

"What package?"

"The compass. From Shipshape. Why did you leave it for me? When were you there?"

Peter shook his head. "I don't know what you're talking about!"

"The—" I stopped myself. It was hardly the most important thing right now, and my voice was hoarse from shouting. "Doesn't matter," I yelled. "Just hold on."

With that, I went back inside the wheelhouse to see how Sal was doing. Her face was as white as Dee's. Her hands were even whiter, gripping the wheel as hard as they could.

"Will you take the wheel for a second?" She turned to me. "I have to talk to Peter."

"Of course!"

"You don't need to do anything," she said. "Just hold this position. Don't let us get any closer. Do you think you can do that?"

I nodded. "But be quick."

She ran outside, leaving me holding a ship's wheel — and our lives — in my hands.

"We need to go back and get help," I said when Sal came back in. Thankfully, she'd taken the wheel from me again. "We'll go back to Porthaven and get the lifeboat people to come out. They'll come over as soon as we tell them what's happened. We just can't do it ourselves."

"You're right," Sal agreed. "Even if we could get the boat onto the shore, how would we get them out of the house?"

"Come on, let's go. It's the only thing we can do."

Sal hesitated. "I know," she said. "It's just . . . I can't bear to leave him here, trapped like that."

I put my hand on her arm. "I'm guessing it'll be an hour, max, by the time the lifeboat gets here," I said. "Peter and Dee look like they're holding on OK. They'll manage an hour."

Sal nodded. "Come on, let's get out of here."

I went back outside. "We can't get anywhere near you," I shouted. "We're going to get the lifeboat. Hold on. We'll be back before you know it."

"Thank you!" Peter called. And, with that, Sal turned the boat around, and we headed back out to the open ocean and the mountainous waves. My stomach dipped and lurched as much as the sea when I thought of going back out there. But we had no choice.

Sal guided us carefully away from the harbor. "I'm going to go out a bit farther before turning, so we don't get thrown against the rocks," she said.

So we headed out again, out toward the open sea. Out on the rodeo horse of an ocean that lifted and dropped us like a giant playing with a toy, booming with every wave like the sky was filled with the biggest bass drum in the world. And then Sal turned the boat and we headed back around the side of the island again. The waves were steeper than ever. The deck was like a swimming pool.

I think I stopped breathing. I was almost ready to say my good-byes to this world. Surely we weren't going to survive this storm.

"Sal! Careful!" I yelled as we rose up high enough to see ahead. A huge rock had come into view not far in front of us. Sal turned the boat sharply to the left and narrowly avoided the rock.

Just as she turned, a blast of wind whistled toward us, grabbed the boat from the back, lifted us high on the waves, and —

And it stopped. All of it. Stopped. The storm, the huge waves, all of it.

One moment, we were driving through blinding rain, raging angry seas, enormous peaks and troughs. The next, the sea calmed, the rain stopped, the wind died. The sun even shone brightly on the water, making it sparkle and twinkle in the light.

We were surrounded by utter stillness and calm. The only movement was the arrow inside the compass, which was spinning furiously.

Sal and I looked at each other. "What on earth happened?" she asked me.

"I have no idea. Can the weather change that drastically, that quickly?" Surely it couldn't. It *couldn't*. So what had happened?

Sal shrugged. "I don't know. But even if it's calm at Luffsands, too, Peter and Dee are still stuck on the roof of a house that's half full of water."

"And Dee's mom is still stuck under a beam."

Sal cranked the engine up to full speed. "Come on," she said. "Let's go and get that lifeboat."

Vera

She wasn't sure how much longer she could bear it. Something would have to give soon. What would it be? The beam? The roof? Her legs?

The house creaked all around her, every sound sending a crackle of fear through her body.

What was that?

She twisted her head to the right just in time to see another piece of ceiling sag and bend and finally break under the weight of water. It sloshed into the pool that was surrounding her. And then a thought hit her, the most terrifying she had had in all these hours. What if *the water level rose above her head before she could tear herself free from the beam?*

She didn't want to drown. Not here, not in her own home. Not when her husband had left in anger, before she'd had one last chance to see his face.

I don't want to die, *she thought. But a second thought came upon her as swiftly as the first.* But I would give my life if it would spare my daughter's.

Diane, up there on the roof, with that boy, trying to get help. She thought she'd heard them shouting a moment ago, but perhaps it was just the screeching of the gulls and the whistling of the wind, and the waves booming through her battered home.

Where had the boy come from? He had arrived at just the wrong moment, hurled from his boat by the wave that had landed him literally at their door. Wrong for him, but right for them. When the bottom floor of the house had been flooded within moments, he was the one who had reached out for her and dragged her up the stairs. And when the beam had fallen, it was he who had grabbed hold of Diane and pulled her to safety. The beam had been heading for Diane's head. If he hadn't been there . . . well, it simply didn't bear thinking about.

After that, everything had happened so fast. The three of them inside the house, the deep booming beats of the sea as it lashed and thrashed at their home. All of them enclosed in the dust and fog and plaster when the ceiling came down. They must all have been knocked unconscious — but for how long? And then, the silence that each of them woke up to as, one by one, they came around and saw what had happened. Those silent hours of unconsciousness — had they cost all three of them their lives?

Had the rescue workers come, and gone, during that time? And how long had it been, anyway? Moments? Hours? If that was when the rescue workers came and they had heard no sound, surely they would believe the house to be empty, all its inhabitants safe.

And then what? Would they come back?

How long could they last like this?

She had already lost all feeling in her legs. What would she lose next?

Chapter Twelve

We tied the boat up on a mooring ring in the next bay around from the harbor. We could probably have brought it into the harbor, but we didn't want to draw attention to ourselves — or to the fact that we were in someone else's boat that we hadn't asked their permission to use.

As soon as the engine died, I hid the key under the bench seat and we scrambled off the boat and ran around to the lifeboat station.

We burst through the door to find a couple of men playing cards at a table. They looked so relaxed that it was as if they didn't even know what was going on just two miles off the coast. Perhaps it was yesterday's news to them and they thought everyone was safe now. But they were wrong!

One of the men turned to us and smiled. "Hello there, girls. Come to have a look around the boat, have you?" He was small and chubby, with sun-bleached blond hair and blue eyes that danced as he spoke.

Sal and I glanced at each other. A look around the boat? Didn't they realize? Didn't they know?

I recovered first. "It's about Luffsands," I said. "There are people still there; they got left behind."

The man looked at his friend. The other man was thinner and bald with a ruddy red face. He leaned forward on the table and squinted at me. "Who got left behind?" he asked. "Left behind from what?"

"From yesterday!" Sal said.

The men exchanged another glance. "Yesterday?" the smaller one repeated. "What happened yesterday?"

"How can you not know?" I squealed. "Please — you have to help them. They're stuck on the top of a house."

"The one on the spit at the far end of the village," Sal added.

The men stood up from their seats. "They must mean the old ruin, Stan," the taller one said. "Kids messing around up there."

"It's not just children. There's a boy and a girl on the roof, but the girl's mom is trapped inside."

"Trapped inside what?" the smaller man — Stan — asked.

"The house!" What was *wrong* with them? Was I talking in a foreign language without realizing it?

"Please," Sal said. "You have to come quickly."

"If you're making this up . . ." the taller man said gravely.

"Of course we're not!" I gasped.

"Look at their faces, Dave," Stan said. "The poor things are terrified. They're not making it up." Then he looked closer at me. "Wait, I've seen you before. Your grandparents run the pub, don't they?"

"Yes, I'm here on vacation." Not exactly the whole truth, but they didn't need to know about our family troubles on top of everything else.

"And you wouldn't want to upset your family by making up stories, would you?" Dave asked.

"We're not making anything up," I insisted. "Please, you have to help."

"These blasted kids playing on the walls. How many times have we warned them?" Dave grumbled as he grabbed a huge waterproof coat and a set of keys.

"Come on, Stan, let's take the inshore boat; it's in the harbor already."

The men were halfway to the door. I ran after them. "We need to come with you," I said. "We have to show you where they are."

Dave turned around. "No can do, I'm afraid," he said. "We're not allowed to take you out in any of the Porthaven boats without permission. One of the things the town council has gotten super firm on since we started advertising vacations here."

"I've got permission!" Sal burst out. She scrabbled in her coat pocket and pulled out a piece of paper. "Look!"

Dave studied it. "So you have," he said.

I stared at Sal.

"We all had to have one for the course," she explained. "It's been in my coat all week from going out on the boat."

Which just left me.

"Hold on a minute," Stan said, coming back inside the lifeboat station. "We've got all those permission slips for the lifeboat open house tomorrow. Maybe there's one for you in there." He grabbed a box from a shelf and started rifling through it.

I stood and watched him for a while. "There won't be one in there," I said miserably. "I haven't asked anyone if I can go to the open house. I didn't even realize that there *was* an open —"

"Got it!" Stan pulled a piece of paper out of the box. "You *have* got permission!"

"*What?* How come? Who from?"

Stan waved the paper at me. "Look," he said. He pointed to the flowing signature: *P. Robinson.* My grandad! I looked at the date. A week ago. He'd signed it before he disappeared!

Stan laughed at me gaping at the paper. "I wouldn't be too shocked," he said. "We had something in the *Times & Echo* last week telling people about the open house. He must have done it on purpose, so you could go. Must have been planning to surprise you."

The thing was, that was exactly the kind of thing Grandad *would* do — organize a special treat without telling me. The thought of him arranging for me to go out on a lifeboat trip as a surprise made me miss him twenty times more than I already was. Except I suddenly realized something — we were only here because he'd gone missing. Had he been planning to invite us to Porthaven at the last minute? To be honest, among all the other unanswered questions, this one wasn't important enough to dwell on. All that mattered was that the lifeboat men could take us to Luffsands.

"So. Are you coming?" Stan asked.

I shook myself and tried to put all thoughts of Grandad out of my head. Peter and Dee were our most pressing concern right now.

"We're coming," Sal and I said in unison — even though my stomach did a slight backward flip as we followed the men out of the lifeboat station. Could I *really* face going out there again?

But then I thought of Peter and Dee, up on that roof, scared to death. They needed us. And anyway, the sea had calmed on the way back. Surely it wouldn't get worse again now.

I glanced at Sal as we headed to the harbor. Her teeth were set tight and her fists clenched as she walked. She obviously relished the thought of going back out to sea as much as I did.

Halfway to the island, I wondered why the lifeboat's engine was banging so loudly. Then I realized it wasn't; it was my heart. We were in the area where the storm had broken out last time.

I held my breath and waited. Nothing happened. The sea stayed calm. I began to breathe again.

But as we came closer to the island and motored

over to the other side, I saw something else. Something even worse than getting caught in a storm out at sea, if that was possible.

Sal looked as stunned as I felt when she turned to me. "The . . . the village . . ." she whispered.

"I know," I whispered back.

The two men were chatting together as they drove. Neither of them seemed to have noticed that anything was wrong. How could they not have seen?

The village had disappeared.

"Where . . . where's it gone?" Sal asked.

The men continued to chat and laugh together as Sal stared, ashen faced, at me.

"Sal, correct me if I'm wrong, OK?" I began. Sal nodded. "OK, so we were here an hour ago. There was a storm, and we couldn't get into the harbor. But we got close enough, and we saw the village. There were a few houses at the front that had almost collapsed, and some of the others had lost windows or roofs. Most of them were flooded up to their second floors. That *is* what we saw, isn't it?"

Sal nodded. "But the houses were *there*," she added. She pointed across at a shoreline that was covered in moss, rubble, seagulls, and nests. A shoreline that looked exactly the same as it had earlier — with just one difference.

All the houses were gone.

I tried to remember something Mom had once told me, about slowing your breathing down when you can feel yourself start to panic. I tried it now.

It didn't work. I gulped in air and tried to arrange my thoughts. What I knew was possible and what I was seeing with my eyes didn't match. That was the simple truth of it.

"Are you girls all right?" Stan asked. "This is where you meant, isn't it?"

I nodded, not trusting myself to say anything sensible if I tried to speak.

"Where were your friends?" Dave asked.

Sal pointed to where we had seen Peter and Dee. I looked across. When we'd been here earlier, they were on the top of a roof of a house that was partially flooded. It was one of three houses on the promontory. Now that same piece of land was about a quarter of the size it had been. It just looked like a large rock, jutting out over the sea below it — and two out of the three houses had completely disappeared.

"Over there," Sal said. She was pointing at a wall. A gable end of a house. That was all that was left standing. As we came at the village from the side, we could see it head-on. It looked like something from a stage set — not real at all. The two downstairs windows had been completely boarded up. The two upper ones were gaping holes. They looked like massive eyes, wide-open but blank and glazed, seeing nothing.

The chimney jutted out at the top. On either side of it, the walls sloped up to the point where Peter and Dee had perched, gripping on to what was now merely a jagged wall, covered in moss.

"OK, we'll moor up and we'll have a look for your friends," Dave said. He drove the boat up to a low rock that jutted out over the sea. It was hardly bigger than a ledge, but just large enough to clamber onto, one at a time. A mooring ring hung from the bottom part of the rock. Stan tied a rope through the ring and leaped off the boat.

"Get off the boat carefully," he said, reaching out to help Sal and then me across.

Once off the boat, I climbed up from the rocky ledge and followed the gravelly path to the flat ground above.

Sal was behind me. "Is this real?" she asked in a whisper.

"I don't know. I don't see how it *can* be. Is there any chance that we're both dreaming?"

The two men had walked up to join us. "OK, do you want to have a look around for your friends?" Stan said. "Check they're not still here?"

I stared at him. What was he talking about? Of *course* they weren't still here! Where exactly did he think they would *be*? Hiding behind a wall, just for the fun of it?

I didn't reply. How could we tell the men what had happened without running the risk of them carting us off to the nearest hospital to have our heads examined?

Sal nudged me. "Great. Thanks," she said to the men.

"Dave and I will check out the dangerous rocky parts. You girls stick to the paths," Stan said. "They're safe enough. The rest isn't. And no climbing on the ruins."

Sal gave them a thumbs-up and a big false smile, then she grabbed my arm and pulled me away to the side.

"Come on, Mia, act normal!" she hissed. "They're going to think we're completely insane!"

"Maybe we *are* completely insane! This isn't *possible*."

"I know," Sal said. "But think about it. If it were just one of us who had seen it, maybe we could have imagined it. But it wasn't. It was both of us, wasn't it?'

The way she looked at me made me realize she wasn't stating a fact; she was asking a question. Asking me to reassure her that I'd experienced the same things as her. That in the space of approximately an hour, what had been a storm-ridden but still-standing village was now little more than a rubble-covered wasteland. And that the house we'd seen Peter and Dee clinging to had become a wall on a tiny promontory jutting out over a perfectly calm sea.

"Yes," I said eventually. "It was both of us."

Sal let out a heavy breath. "OK. Well, that's one good thing," she said. "We can't *both* be going crazy. But what does that prove? And how does it get us any nearer to finding Peter and Dee?"

I kicked at a pile of stones at my feet while I tried to think. "I've no idea," I admitted. "But I don't think we should tell Dave and Stan the truth. For one thing, they'll never believe us."

"And for another, they'll think we're nuisance kids who are making the whole thing up," Sal added.

"Exactly."

"So what *do* we do?" she asked.

"Let's just look around the place, see if we can find any clues, anything that helps us to make sense of any of this."

"OK," she said, and we headed off toward what remained of Dee's house at the far end of the village.

* * *

I walked around, almost tiptoeing in the silence of this abandoned and ruined place. I felt like someone in a TV drama about lone survivors in a postapocalyptic world. There was no human life here.

I'd never felt such silence. I don't just mean an absence of sound. It was as though the silence itself were part of the place, filling it up louder than sound could ever do.

The ground below my feet was springy with moss and grass; I almost bounced as I walked. On either side of the spongy path, there were piles and piles of rubble and stones. Down below, the water lapped gently on the rocks. An occasional soft *BOOM!* echoed in the silence as a stronger wave hit the hollow under a massive rock that jutted out over the sea. It had a hole on its underside, as though the sea itself had reared up and taken a bite.

Following the path back toward the cliff that rose up behind us, I came to another wall. This one had collapsed in stages. It looked like a staircase, as if you could start at the top of the wall and climb down it one step at a time. It had a hole in it that must have been a door at some point. I walked around to the back of the wall and looked through the gap. The huge expanse of sea stared silently back at me.

I moved on.

In front of the wall, a single snowdrop poked up

from among the rubble. Faded, grayish-white, and drooping, its closed-up buds hung limply, dying and forgotten, like everything else here.

Farther along, I disturbed a group of squawking seagulls. They flew off as I came near, and landed a little farther away.

The birds were clearly the only residents of this place. What stories would they tell, if they could? What had they seen? And when had they seen it? Had the storm really happened yesterday, or had something completely inexplicable — something I couldn't even put into words — happened here?

I wished the seagulls could tell me.

"Mia!" Sal broke my daydream.

I turned around. "What?"

She pointed at the ground a little way ahead of me and I gasped. The path ended abruptly and a rickety fence stopped us from going any farther. Beyond it, there was a chasm in the rock. You couldn't see it from farther away, but if we had taken another couple of steps, we would have walked right off the edge, plunging down to where the sea was quietly splashing around, a long, long way below.

I let out a heavy breath. "Jeepers," I breathed, not really able to think of anything more intelligent to say.

Sal came up beside me. "How do we get to the house?" she asked.

The wall, the only remaining piece of Dee's house, was on the other side of the chasm — and there was absolutely no way of getting across it.

"We don't."

"But —"

"Sal, what difference does it make? They're not there. The *house* is hardly there, and we can see all the way through it from here — through those great big gaping holes in the side. It's empty! It's dead and deserted, like this whole place."

I could feel my voice rising. I took a breath and added more gently, "Sal, there's no one here. And, more to the point, there's been no one here for *years*."

"But it doesn't make *sense*," Sal insisted.

"I know it doesn't. But it's true. Look around. It's a completely abandoned, destroyed, deserted place."

I turned around in a full circle to survey my surroundings and try to convince myself they were real. That was when I noticed something that made me catch my breath, right over at the edge of the spit of land, just in front of where we stood. I walked across to take a closer look.

It was a crumbling low wall, like others all around the

place, but with one difference: it was pink. A very faded pink, but you could clearly see the color, which stood out among the gray. The wall came up about as high as my knees and was probably once the back corner of a house.

I remembered Dee telling me about the family who had owned this house. I couldn't recall their names, but I remembered what she'd said. The couple who lived here had just painted the place pink because their young daughter had insisted on it.

This pink had been painted a long time ago.

Where was the family now? What had happened to them? What had happened to all of it? How was any of this possible?

My heart felt heavy, and I wasn't sure how much more of this I could take.

"Sal, let's go back," I said.

She just nodded without saying anything. That was when I realized how much harder this must be for her than for me. An hour ago, we were filled with hope that we were about to bring her brother home; now he seemed more lost than ever.

"We'll find him," I said, touching her arm as we walked. "We'll bring him home."

Sal just nodded and swallowed. We didn't say anything else till we got back to the lifeboat.

Chapter Thirteen

The men were waiting for us. "So, you want to tell us the truth about your friends?" Dave asked. "They weren't here at all, really, were they?"

We didn't reply. How could we? There was nothing we could say that would make sense — or that the men would believe.

"You know we're an emergency service, don't you?" Stan said as we clambered aboard and Dave started the engine.

"What do you mean?" I asked.

"I mean, it's probably best if you don't waste our time again."

I looked at his face to see if he was angry, but he'd turned away to pull a fender over the side of the boat.

"We're not going to report you this time," he went on as we started chugging away from the island. "But next time you're craving a boat trip, it's best if you ask one of the fishermen to give you a ride. What if we'd had a real emergency come in while we were taking you girls out on a joyride?"

"A joyride?" I gasped. "You think this was a *joyride*?"

Stan shrugged. "OK, to be fair, I can't say either of you looks exactly filled with joy. Well, what *was* it about, then?"

I opened my mouth to reply and caught Sal's eye before I began. She quickly shook her head: *don't tell them.*

"I'm really sorry," I said. "It wasn't a joyride, and we weren't tricking you. But we were wrong. We thought our friends were over there, but we hadn't already been there like we said."

"We thought if we said we'd been there and seen them, you'd be more likely to come," Sal added.

Stan looked at us, studying each of our faces— probably to see if we were lying. I don't know what he saw there, but whatever it was, he spoke more gently. "All right," he said. "Like I said, you're not in trouble."

No, but Peter and Dee still are.

"Just be honest next time, OK?"

"OK. Sorry," I said again.

"Go and check where your friends are staying. You'll probably find they're at home safe and sound," Stan finished.

"Probably," I said woodenly.

The rest of the journey back was calm and uneventful. Soon, Dave was pulling the boat back into the harbor and Stan stood up to get ready with the ropes.

"Now, go and find your friends and have a nice day," he said. "No more silly stories, OK?"

"No more silly stories," I repeated.

"We're sorry," Sal added.

"All right. Good girls." Stan slung the rope over a cleat and reached out to help us off the boat. "Off you go, now. And try to cheer up a bit, eh? Porthaven's not the worst place in the world to spend your vacation, you know."

We got off the boat and left Dave and Stan sorting out ropes and engines. We didn't start talking till we were sure we were out of earshot. Then Sal stopped and turned to me.

"Now what do we do?" she asked.

"I was about to ask you the same thing. Do you think we should go back to the pub?"

She shook her head. "I can't face it. What would we say? *Hey, we saw Peter. He was hanging off the roof of a flooded house in the middle of a terrible storm. So we got the rescue boat out to get him, and guess what! He wasn't there anymore! And neither was the house. Or the village.* That'd go over well, don't you think?"

"Exactly. We can't tell your parents. We can't tell *anyone.* They'll think we're bonkers."

"Or that we made it up, like the lifeboat men did."

"Right. And to be fair, who could blame them?" I added. "If I heard someone say that, *I'd* think they'd either made it up or lost their mind, for sure."

"So what *do* we do?" Sal asked.

I thought for a moment. "We need to find out what's going on," I said. Possibly stating the obvious, but what else *could* we do?

"I agree. But how?"

I shrugged. "Normally I'd say let's look up a bunch of stuff on the Internet—but we can't."

"Why not?"

I opened my arms to take in all of Porthaven. "This place," I said. "I don't know anywhere around here that gets a signal."

Sal stared at me. "I do," she said. "Come on." And then she hurried off.

I quickly caught up with her. "Where are we going?" I asked.

Sal answered without looking at me. "Our rental apartment. It has a computer and a Wi-Fi connection. It was what made Dad choose that apartment — he's addicted to the Internet. He thinks the sky will fall if he doesn't go online at least twenty times a day."

"Awesome!" An actual Internet signal! I could hardly believe it. I was going to reenter the twenty-first century for the first time in a week.

Sal suddenly stopped walking. "What if my parents are still there?" she asked.

I thought for a moment. "We ask if we can use the computer, but we don't tell them what it's for," I said.

"So what *do* we say?"

"Just that you've come to pack up your things, and I've come to help you, and I want to look up a song on the Internet or something."

"OK," Sal agreed. "They've probably gotten their stuff together and gone back to the pub by now anyway."

"Have you got a key?" I asked as we approached the apartment.

"Don't need one. The door is number coded."

As Sal punched in the numbers, part of me wondered what we were doing. What exactly were we going to look up online? And what was it going to tell us? It wasn't as if Peter was likely to have disappeared without a trace, and then sent us an e-mail telling us where we could find him!

I fought the doubts away. At least we were doing *something*. It might not be much of a plan, but it was the only one we had.

I pulled up a chair next to Sal and listened to the computer slowly whir into action. Her parents had come and gone and the place was empty, apart from Sal's room. Most of her stuff was in a small suitcase that was open on the bed, with a note lying on top.

We've packed most of your things for you. Come over to the pub as soon as you're ready.
Love you, Mom & Dad

Finally, the computer was up and running. It hummed quietly while we tried to figure out exactly what to type.

Sal's fingers hovered over the keyboard. She looked at me.

"Why don't you see if there's a coastwatch station or something for this area?" I suggested. "Maybe they'll have a list of people who have been rescued."

She brought up a search engine and typed "Porthaven Coastwatch."

After about five minutes of scrolling and reading through all sorts of technical jargon, we found it—a list of recent events that had taken place in this area. I held my breath as the page loaded.

"Nothing," Sal said.

I read everything on the screen. The last entry was more than a week ago.

Sal stared at the computer. "Now what?"

"Look at the weather reports," I suggested. "See if there's anything about that freak storm."

"Good idea."

Sal hit a few keys and we tried a few weather pages. Again we couldn't find anything useful. There were no reports of storms in more than a month.

"Why is there nothing about it?" Sal asked.

"I don't know. Too recent, maybe?"

"Too recent? But isn't that supposed to be the whole point of the Internet? You can read about things the second they've happened."

"I know, I don't get it," I said. And then I realized what we should be looking for. It was obvious. So obvious that we'd looked right past it; or we'd simply been too scared of what we might see if we tried it. Either way, it was the only thing I could think of that might give us any answers.

"Sal."

She turned to me.

I nodded at the keyboard. "Just put in 'Luffsands.'"

A line of text at the top of the page said that there were 451,623 results for Luffsands. Below it, the screen was filled with links to tons of web pages.

"Where do we start?" Sal asked.

I shrugged. "The first one?"

She clicked on the top link. It led us to a page from the Wildlife Trust, full of statistics about birdlife found on the island.

Sal went back to the search engine and tried the next one. The page took forever to open. When it finally did, it was blank except for a line of small black text at the top: "Link Not Found. Error 5201."

"This is stupid," Sal said, flopping back in her chair. "We're not getting anywhere."

I leaned over and reached for the mouse. "Let's try this one." I scrolled to the bottom of the page and hit the last link.

"It's a newspaper article," I said as the page loaded.

"And look," Sal added. "It's got today's date. We're getting somewhere at last." She hit a button to enlarge the window and we read the article together.

Luffsands was hit yesterday by one of the worst storms in living history.

The village, home to sixty-seven families, was left in ruins by a combination of the fiercest northeasterly winds on record and the highest tide of the year.

Seven houses were completely destroyed. Many others were left without roofs, windows, or floors. Forecasters are predicting even worse gales over the coming days. If their timing combines with the tide as disastrously as yesterday's storm, the destruction could be even more devastating.

Nigel Cannister, from the Eastern Coastwatch Station, said, "We've conducted three search and rescue missions so far, and we believe we've gotten all the residents out. The conditions our men have been working in have been exceptionally difficult, and yesterday's rescue mission had to be halted when an entire piece of land collapsed into the sea. We will be returning to make absolutely sure no one has been left behind, once it is safe to do so."

Mr. Cannister went on. "We are advising that no one attempts to return to the island until we have officially given the all clear. Unfortunately, we do not expect to be able to do this anytime soon. If the forecasters are correct, we anticipate that the entire village could go the same way as the front houses. In other words, by the end of this week, there may be no village to return to.

The article ended there. Underneath it was a photograph. It was small and quite blurry, but you could see clearly what it was — Luffsands, taken from the sea. The Luffsands we had seen this morning, the first time we went. The Luffsands where Dee's house was still standing. Where about fifty houses were still standing.

Sal and I stared at the screen.

"I don't get it," Sal said. "The article's from today. It says the storm was yesterday."

"Which means that what we saw when we went across on our own was *real*," I said.

"Exactly. So why does no one else seem to know anything about it? And how come it had all completely changed when we went back?"

I scrolled down the page. There was another line of text at the bottom of the newspaper article, but it was too small to read.

Sal enlarged it, and we both read what it said.

"That's why," I said. Then I looked at her and she looked at me. Neither of us had any words.

The article *was* today's date: February 23. But there was one small difference.

It was February 23 — fifty years ago.

Chapter Fourteen

I don't know how long I stared at that date. I don't know why I kept on staring, either. Was I expecting it to change? Suddenly morph into something that made sense?

Sal broke into my thoughts. "Look," she said. "There's another article underneath it."

This one was dated late March, the same year.

Former residents of Luffsands yesterday visited the remains of their village, in an attempt to salvage anything that remained of their former homes.

The village's seventy-nine houses were all destroyed in severe storms just over four weeks ago. Miraculously, there were no fatalities, although the lives that were left in tatters will take many years to rebuild.

The visit was the first time residents had been able to return, and it took place after the local coastwatch finally gave the all clear. After weeks of landslides and collapses, Luffsands has now been declared safe to visit—but only under strict supervision from the coastwatch.

Residents took the opportunity to return to their former homes and search through wreckage in an attempt to rescue any personal belongings that had not been washed away by the tides following last month's storms.

Anyone wishing to contribute to the Luffsands Residents' Fund should get in touch with the newspaper.

There was a photograph underneath the article. Sal clicked on it to enlarge the picture.

The first thing I noticed was that it was completely different from the photograph with the first article. That one had been the Luffsands we had seen this morning when we'd shouted across to Peter and Dee. This one was the Luffsands we had seen an hour later, with the lifeboat men. No houses standing. Dee's house nothing more than a wall, perched on the tip of a promontory, resolutely sticking out over the sea.

Two photographs, a month apart—and yet we'd seen both of these scenes in the space of one morning.

But that wasn't the most shocking thing about the picture. In fact, that was *nothing* compared to what I was about to see.

There were about twenty people in the shot. Most of them were in the background, bent over, examining the wreckage of their former homes. In the foreground, six people huddled together, looking toward the camera. The photographer clearly hadn't suggested that anyone smile. Their faces were heavy and pained. At the end of the group, a woman on crutches leaned heavily on a boy standing next to her.

I stared at the boy. Then I checked the date on the top of the newspaper. It was *definitely* from fifty years ago. And it was *definitely* impossible.

"The boy . . ." I said, unable to finish.

There was no need. Sal was staring too. "I know," she said. "It can't be."

But it was. The boy staring glumly into the

camera — in a photograph that was taken fifty years ago — was Peter.

"Mia, I've got to get out of here," Sal gasped. She looked as if she had literally seen a ghost. Maybe she had.

"Me too," I said. "Grab your things and let's go."

I shut down the computer while Sal packed the last of her stuff. Then we let ourselves out of the apartment and made our way along the front, toward the pub.

We didn't speak as we walked. There weren't any words that could make sense of all the things that had happened today. And there was no way either of us could even think about anything else, not after what we'd seen, so the only option was silence.

"Mia, can we sit here for a bit?" Sal asked as we came to a bench looking out over the harbor. "I can't face seeing anyone yet."

We sat down and looked out at the sea, the calm water, the boats bobbing gently in the harbor. Was any of this real? Were we in some kind of a dream? I tried to figure out at which point I might have fallen asleep. It was the closest I'd come to an explanation — but then Sal brought me back to the present.

"I think we should tell our families," she said.

"Yeah," I agreed.

"They'll think we're crazy," she added.

"I know. Maybe we are. It's certainly the best explanation I've managed to come up with so far."

Sal tried to smile.

"But we should tell them, either way," I went on. "Whatever's going on here, whether we're losing our minds, or something unbelievably weird is happening, I think we need help with it. We can't do it on our own anymore."

"I know," Sal agreed. "We'll tell them everything, then?"

I nodded. "Everything."

"And if they don't believe us?"

"If they don't believe us, we haven't lost anything. But at least we'll get it off our chests. They've been around longer than we have. They might have some ideas about what's going on."

"I doubt it," Sal said quietly. "I don't think there's *any* explanation for what's going on."

"No, probably not," I agreed.

"But whatever it is, it's too big for us," she said.

"Exactly."

We got up to leave and turned in the direction of the pub. As we did, I walked smack-dab into a man coming toward us.

"Sorry," I said automatically.

He stopped and looked at me. His clothes looked dirty. His eyes were unfocused and wild. Drunk, probably. Then he looked at my coat. I was still wearing Peter's yellow coat that we'd found inside the boat.

"I've got one of them," he said, pointing at the coat. Great. A drunk man who found it interesting that he also possessed a coat. Exactly what we needed right then. "Not as nice as that one, though."

"That's lovely," I said, giving him a *thanks-for-the-info-but-we-really-must-be-on-our-way-now* kind of smile.

"Left it on my boat," he added.

I couldn't put my finger on it, but something about his words made me feel as if something unpleasant had just crept along the back of my neck.

The feeling multiplied by about a million with his *next* words.

"Lost the boat, though, didn't I?" he said. "Along with my mind, it seems. Slept in a hut last night. No one'd take me home. Looked at me as if I were crazy when I told them where I lived. Laughed at me when I said my boat had disappeared into thin air. But it's true. Strange, but darned well true as can be."

I stared at him. The way he was talking, he sounded like us!

The man moved away. "Anyway, see you, then," he said.

"Wait!" I called before I could stop myself.

"What are you doing?" Sal hissed. "He's more crazy than *we* are! *And* he's drunk!"

"I don't think he is," I whispered. "Just bear with me, OK?"

The man swung around. As he did so, something flashed just above the V-neck of his sweater. A necklace. *An anchor pendant.* The thing Dee's dad always wore when he went fishing!

I was right! I swallowed hard, took a breath, and said, "I think we might have found your boat."

"What?" the man said.

"*What?*" Sal said.

"It's in the first bay around the corner from here," I went on. "Tied up on a mooring ring. The key is in the usual place."

The man took a step closer to me and looked into my eyes. "Are you making fun of me, young lady?"

I shook my head hard. I wasn't going to try to explain. He'd *definitely* think I was making fun of him if I did. "I promise I'm telling the truth," I said. "Just go."

The man looked at me a moment longer, and then

he nodded his head. "All right, then," he said. "I will." And he turned to leave.

"Wait!" I called again. I grabbed Dee's diary from inside my bag and turned to Sal. "Have you got a pen?"

She rummaged around in her bag before pulling out a ballpoint pen. "I don't know what you're —" she began.

I cut her off. "I'll explain later." *If I can,* I added silently. And then I scribbled a quick note.

> Dee, I'm sorry we didn't get to meet up. We will one day — I hope. Just look after yourself.
> Love from your friend,
> Mia

I closed the diary and held it out to the man. "Here, take this with you," I said.

He looked at the book and took it from me. And then, without another word, he set off toward the bay where we'd left the boat, and we made our way back to the pub.

As we arrived at the pub, I realized I was shaking.

"What will we tell them?" Sal whispered.

"The truth, as we agreed," I said, hoping she hadn't heard the quiver in my voice. "We tell them everything."

I pushed the door open and we crept inside. The lounge was almost empty. Three men sat at the bar, drinking pints and talking in gruff voices. A couple was at a table in the window, drinking coffee and eating cookies. How could they sit there calmly doing that while our world had been turned upside down and inside out?

The pub felt so normal. Suddenly I realized what a mess I must look like in comparison.

I still had Peter's oversize fisherman's coat on. And my hair was all over the place. I'd put it up in a ponytail this morning, but the storm had pulled half of it out, and it had stayed like that ever since. Fixing my hair had hardly been a priority. Sal looked pretty bedraggled too.

"Let's go and freshen up a bit," I said to Sal. "Come up with me, and then we'll find the others."

Sal started to follow me, but we had only gotten halfway across the lounge when the door behind the bar opened and Gran came in.

She didn't see us at first. She was looking behind her, calling something over her shoulder as she swung through the door. Then she nodded to the men and took the pint glass one of them was holding out to her. She turned toward the tap at the end of the bar.

And then she glanced across at us, and froze.

As she stared, I met her gaze and realized, for the

first time ever, that she looked old. Her skin seemed to sag on her cheeks. Her eyes were dark and hollow. Her neck was creased with tiny lines.

And now, on top of that, her face had turned gray.

She put down the glass she had just taken from the fisherman, without taking her eyes off me. Then she lifted the flap at the end of the bar and walked toward us.

Still staring at me, she crossed the lounge and came to stand in front of me. Her eyes were shining and wet. What was going on?

Gran reached for my arm, feeling the coat I still had on. She touched it as though it were the first time she'd ever seen a yellow fisherman's coat. Then she reached up and stroked my matted, sodden hair. She smoothed back a strand that had been plastered to my forehead, and in a voice husky with emotion, she said, "It was you."

What was she talking about? *What* was me? Was I in trouble? Did she know about us taking the boat?

Before I had a chance to think of a reply, she went on, "Was it? Am I right? Tell me it was you," she said. "Or have I gotten so old, so desperate, and so confused that I really am losing my mind?"

I had no idea what she was talking about. Maybe she *was* losing her mind. I knew that stress could do that to people, and Gran had certainly been stressed for the last week.

"Gran, I don't —" I began.

She put a hand to my lips. "Wait," she said. "Don't say anything else."

Then she turned and walked away. Flinging the door behind the bar open, she called to Mom, "Take over at the bar for a minute, will you, dear?" and ran upstairs.

I looked at Sal.

"What on earth was that about?" she asked.

"I've got no idea."

"Do you think someone's told her about us taking the boat? She wouldn't report us or anything, would she?"

"No way. Gran wouldn't do that."

But if she hadn't gone upstairs to phone the police and tell them about her granddaughter's antics on a boat she had no permission to use, what *was* she doing? And what had she meant? Why had she looked at me so strangely? There was something about the way she'd stared at me, and at my coat, touched my hair — it wasn't normal. In fact, it was so *un*-normal that everything else could wait.

"Look, can you wait here for a bit?" I asked Sal. "I need to find out what's going on."

With that, I left Sal in the pub, barged past Mom, who was just coming in, and ran upstairs to talk to Gran.

I knocked on her bedroom door. "Gran?" No reply. I pushed open the door. "Gran? Are you in here?" I called as I looked around. Her bedroom was empty.

Then I heard a noise upstairs. She was in Grandad's study. What was she doing in there?

I charged up the stairs and found her kneeling on the floor. She didn't even look up when I came in. She was rummaging so deeply in a box that her head was practically inside it.

"Gran?"

"One second." She carried on foraging in the box without looking up. "It's here somewhere, I know it is," she muttered, lifting out bundles of books and papers and dumping them on the floor beside her as she delved deeper.

And then she stopped. Lifting out a small cardboard box, she looked at me. "Found it," she said.

Then, finally, she met my eyes. "It was the coat," she said, answering the question I wasn't asking out loud. "I recognized it. And your hair. You look exactly the same."

"The same as what?" I asked.

"I couldn't see your face. Not through all that rain." She laughed softly, staring into the distance as if watching her own memories being replayed. "What if I had?" Then she turned back to me. "But the picture was etched in my mind as if it had been carved there. The wild, wet hair. The coat." She stopped and shook her head. "Here," she said. She took the lid off the box and held it out to me.

The box was filled with cream-colored tissue paper. I looked down at the tissue paper and the box, and I wondered, briefly, what was inside it. What was so important that Gran had charged up here to find it? What was it about this box that had made her eyes sparkle with something I couldn't possibly define, but I knew I'd never seen before? And what was it that made her hand tremble as she pushed the box into my palms?

As I took it from her, the room fell away from us. It was as if there were nothing in the world but the two of us. Suddenly I was scared.

"What is it?" I asked.

Gran held my eyes. "Just open it," she said softly.

I pulled the tissue paper away. When I saw what was wrapped inside it, I almost dropped the box.

It was Dee's diary.

Chapter Fifteen

I shoved the box back at Gran, pushing it into her hands as though it had burned my fingers. "That's impossible!" I said.

It *couldn't* be real. I'd only just given it away! Minutes ago!

Gran took the box back from me and pulled the book out. Maybe it was a copy. Maybe it was just a coincidence. Maybe . . .

"Read the last entry," Gran said, passing the book to me.

I opened it up. As I flipped toward the end, I saw my writing. My words. The words I had written moments earlier, before giving the book to Dee's dad. But now the ink was faded, as if it had been written years ago.

The room began to spin.

I grabbed hold of the chair at Grandad's desk, pulled it out, and sat down, feeling as wooden as the chair itself.

"The page after that," Gran said.

I turned the page, to see writing that in the last week had become almost as familiar to me as my own.

Dee's writing.

Gosh, I've just realized it's been more than a month since I last wrote. Well, obviously I haven't felt like writing a diary lately. Life has involved a lot more important things than scribbling my own self-indulgent thoughts and feelings down on paper.

Things like survival.

Honestly, those first couple of days, I really thought our time was up. When I think about it now, I can hardly believe what we went through. We spent all those hours clinging to the roof of a house that turned out to be less than a day from total collapse. If Father hadn't come back when he did. If he hadn't been as experienced on the sea, and known the tiny nook at the edge of the harbor where he could still moor up the boat . . .

But he did. That's all that matters. That and the fact that Mother survived. The doctors told us yesterday that she will almost certainly never walk unaided again. She put on a brave smile, like she always does, and told us she was just happy to be alive. I have to admit, there were a few hours when I doubted if even that would be the case, and so I see her point. But still . . .

No. I won't do it. I won't allow myself feelings of self-pity. I'll never do it again. It's time for me to be the strong one now. Father is like a broken man. The home he adored has been washed into the sea. The boat that was his livelihood is up for sale, as he can no longer bring himself to go out in her. And my mother will never walk — and perhaps never laugh — again.

Now I have to be the one to look after this family. I will do everything I can to get all of us looking forward again.

There was an advertisement in the newspaper today. The local pub in our new town needs a landlord. Perhaps Father could do it.

I'm going to take him the ad later. I'll help. And Pip will, too.

Pip. I cannot believe that a month ago, I didn't know him. Now he is like a second self to me. Between us, I know we can do it. We can get this family back on its feet.

I have only one regret. One thought that pulls at my heart so hard it pains my chest.

Mia. She sent me my lovely boy. She directed my father back home. With both of these things, she saved me from death, gave us all another chance at life. And I never had the chance to thank her.

If I could be granted one wish, it would be simply that — to stand in front of her and say "thank you"

The diary entry ended there. It was the last one in the book. I didn't know what to think, let alone what to say. My mind was swimming, crammed full of thoughts, and at the same time as blank as the last pages of Dee's diary.

I looked up at Gran.

Her eyes were shiny and misty. "I've got that chance, now, haven't I?" she whispered. "However impossible it may be, it's true, isn't it? I can finally say thank you."

And just like that, I knew I couldn't handle this. Any of it. I had to get out of there.

I stood up, almost falling over in the process. The room was spinning; I was pretty sure I was going to be sick. "I've got to go," I said.

And then I turned and ran down the stairs, out to the back of the pub. Flake looked up and wagged his shaggy tail at me as I came into the kitchen.

Flake. Normal, happy, uncomplicated Flake.

"I could do with having you around," I said, and quickly clipped on his leash.

And then, before anyone could stop us, I unlatched the back door, took Flake, and got the heck away from there. Away from Gran, the pub, the diary, and everything else about my world that had suddenly gone absolutely, totally, impossibly crazy.

It had started raining. I didn't care. I didn't even feel it. I didn't feel anything.

I sat on a bench and stared out to sea, Flake leaning gently against my legs as I tried to get my head into some sort of state where I could begin to make sense of my thoughts.

Where was I supposed to start?

"Mia." A voice interrupted my attempt at thinking. I turned to see Sal running toward me.

"What happened to you?" she asked, coming over to stand in front of me. "What's up with your gran? Did you tell her?"

I held up a hand to ward off any more questions. "Which one do you want me to answer first?"

Sal took a breath. "Just, I thought we were telling our families. Next thing I know, you've disappeared, your gran's disappeared, your mom's asking where you both are and what's going on, and I'm standing there opening and closing my mouth like a goldfish."

"I'm sorry."

Sal looked at me for a moment, then sat down on the bench next to me. "No. I'm sorry," she said. "Are you OK? You look awful."

"Thanks."

"I mean . . . Jeez, I'm not doing very well here, am I?"

I shook my head. "It's not you. It's —"

"What? What happened with your gran?" Sal asked again. "Do you want to tell me?"

Did I? That was a good question. Would Sal think we were *all* crazy if I did? Then again, she'd shared in half the bizarre things that had happened already.

Maybe she was the only person I *could* tell without worrying about what she thought. Maybe she was the only person who could help me figure any of this out.

"Yes," I said. "I want to tell you."

Sal listened while I emptied my brain of everything that was in it. After that, we didn't say anything for a while. We just sat together, watching the waves come in, lapping against the sand, rocking the boats in the harbor. It all looked so peaceful and calm and gentle — it was such a lie.

Sal sat back and let out a breath. "Wow," she said eventually.

"I know."

"So your gran . . ."

"And Dee . . ."

Sal turned to me. "They're . . ."

She couldn't say the words. I didn't blame her. You try it. Think of the craziest thought you could ever have, then imagine saying it out loud to someone as a serious possibility without feeling ridiculous beyond belief.

It's not easy, is it?

I decided to save Sal the effort of trying. "Gran and Dee are the same person," I said flatly.

There. I'd done it. I'd said the impossible words that we both knew were somehow true.

We sat in silence. I felt as though the words were dancing in front of me, bouncing around in the air while I tried to hold on to them and pull them into some sort of recognizable shape. I couldn't.

"But there must be — what — fifty years between them," Sal said eventually.

"Yep."

Wait! She was right! *Fifty years.* "Sal, the article about Luffsands!"

"What about it?"

"It was fifty years old, wasn't it?"

"Yes, but —"

"Gran turned sixty-three this year. Dee's thirteen. There are *exactly* fifty years between them, and the storm happened exactly fifty years ago."

"What are you saying?" Sal asked in a whisper.

I shook my head. "I don't know . . . but there's something weird going on."

"You *think*?"

"No, I mean . . . Look, I feel like a complete idiot saying this out loud, but I'm going to anyway, OK? And you're not to laugh at me or tell me I'm crazy."

"I'm not going to do that, Mia. If you're crazy, I am too. I've seen all this stuff as well."

"OK." I took a breath. "So, firstly, I think it's got something to do with the boat."

"The boat? How?"

"I sent notes to Dee on her dad's boat, and if we're right about Dee and Gran being the same person, then those notes were traveling back in time fifty years."

"OK," Sal said slowly.

"Then you and I went to Luffsands on the same boat and found ourselves in the middle of a storm — a storm that happened fifty years ago."

"So the boat somehow makes you travel backward and forward fifty years in time?"

"Or maybe it's the compass," I said, thinking out loud.

"The way it went spinning like that," Sal added.

"Exactly." There was something in all this, but it was beyond the reach of my thoughts. I just couldn't get my brain to add it all together into something that worked.

I shrugged. What did I have to lose? If I'd already lost my mind, Sal was there with me. "Look, I know it's completely cr —"

"No, you're right," Sal said. "That's what's happened

to Peter! That's why he hasn't come home to us. He's gone back in time — and now that that man's taken his boat, we've got no way of bringing him back again."

"That man . . . Dee's dad," I said.

"Mia," Sal said, so quietly her voice was like a wisp of wind ruffling a calm sea.

"What?"

"If Dee is your gran, and that man was her father . . ."

"Yes?"

Sal swallowed. "Then who is Peter?"

I was about to answer, but two things stopped me. The first was that I couldn't make my brain piece together an answer. Or I could, but this time I knew that if I did, I was *really* going to go crazy!

The second was the sound of shuffling footsteps behind us.

I turned my head as the footsteps came closer. I looked up. Right in front of my eyes was the last person I expected to see, and the one who had been at the center of all my thoughts for a week.

I leaped off the bench and threw my arms around him.

"Grandad!"

Peter

He sat at the dining room table with his homework. His mom was upstairs, vacuuming. His dad was still in bed. His sister, Sal, was in the kitchen, getting a snack to eat in front of the television.

Logarithms. Whoever invented logarithms? And why? What job was he ever likely to get that would depend on his knowing how many times to multiply a factor of three?

Still, Peter had never handed his homework in late, and never been in trouble, so he persevered. That was simply the kind of boy he was — and everyone knew it. He was one of the few who was liked as much by the teachers as he was by his fellow pupils. And he wasn't about to let a mind-bending equation change that.

So he kept his head down and concentrated on the mass of swirling numbers and formulas. If he got it all done now, he'd have the rest of the weekend to do what he wanted without it hanging over him.

But when he heard a soft "thud" coming from the hallway, his mind was sufficiently open to distraction that he was out of his chair in a flash.

He stood in the hallway and looked around. Nothing. He opened the porch door and looked down at the mat. There was something lying facedown on the floor—a magazine or pamphlet.

Peter bent down to pick it up. It was a travel brochure for a place he'd never heard of. "Come Fishing in Porthaven" it said on the front.

Fishing? Having lived in a city his whole life, fishing was not something that had ever entered his thoughts. In fact, he'd never even been on a boat! Where was Porthaven anyway? And who had delivered the brochure? The mail carrier had already come.

Curious, he opened the front door, expecting to see a teenager with a big satchel over his shoulder delivering the brochures to every house on the street. But there was no one delivering anything. The only person in sight on the street at all was a man with his back to Peter, right at the end of the road.

Peter watched him, registered that he seemed quite old, that he was wearing a big wool coat, that his hair was wispy and windblown, and that he seemed in a hurry to get away.

Just as the man was about to turn the corner, he stopped, as if he weren't sure which direction to take. And then, very slowly, he turned back and looked down the road. His eyes met Peter's. For the briefest of instants, the man and the boy locked eyes.

The next moment, Peter was struck by a blinding headache so fierce it made him scrunch his eyes closed and clutch his head. What was it? A migraine? Peter had never had one, so he didn't know what they were like. All he knew was that he'd never felt pain like this in his life.

Still holding on to his head, Peter stumbled into the house. As he grew more agitated, a blotchy red rash crept around his neck. "Mom!" he called. Then he fell to his knees and waited for the pain to recede.

The mystery headache lasted for the rest of the day. Peter could do nothing that afternoon but lie on his bed in the dark.

No football. Football was the only reason Saturdays existed as far as Peter was concerned. But he had no choice.

He struggled down to join his family for dinner.

"This place looks absolutely heavenly," his mom murmured, flipping through the brochure as she munched on an apple.

His dad frowned. "Can we afford it?" he asked. "Now that I've been made part-time and layoffs are looming, I could be out of a job by this time next month."

"All the more reason to take a vacation now," Peter's mom insisted.

His dad leaned over to look at the brochure. "True enough," he said. "And to be honest, I've always wanted to take a fishing vacation. What do you think, kids?"

Peter shrugged. "Whatever," he said. He'd taken some aspirin but could still barely open his eyes without searing pain crashing through his head.

"I prefer horseback riding myself," Sal said before getting up from the table and taking her plate to the sink.

"Ooh, look, they've got dates during spring break," Mom pointed out. "We'd been wondering what to do then."

Dad kissed his wife on the forehead and picked up the brochure as Peter finished his dinner and excused himself from the table. The pain was getting bad again and he needed darkness and quiet.

"Well, let's not wonder anymore," his dad was saying, heading for the phone as Peter headed back to his bed.

"Let's go fishing in Porthaven."

Chapter Sixteen

Grandad held me tightly for a couple of seconds, then took hold of my hands and pried them off his neck.

As I moved away, I saw that someone else had come out of the pub and was halfway toward us. Gran!

She was staring across at Grandad, her eyes as shiny as glass, her hands clenched together. He was staring back at her, too. Their gaze was like electricity: it almost crackled. Grandad stood as still as the statue on the promenade and waited for Gran to join us.

Then he wrapped his hands around hers. "Diane, I'm sorry I disappeared into thin air like that," he said. "But I had to do it."

Gran swallowed and nodded. She took one of her hands away from his. For a moment, I thought she was going to change her mind and walk off again. *No — please don't! Hear him out!* I wanted to shout.

But she didn't leave. Instead, she lifted her hand to his cheek and stroked his face. "I know that now," she whispered.

Grandad tilted his head. "You know?" he repeated.

"You know *what*?" I added.

Gran turned to me, as if she'd only just noticed I was there. Then she smiled. "Everything," she said.

"But —" Grandad began.

She put a finger on his lips to stop him saying any more. "I think in some part of me, I always knew," she went on. "But I didn't want to admit it, in case it made it all go away. In case it made *you* go away."

Grandad wrapped his arms around Gran, pulling her close. "I love you so much," he said, kissing her neck.

Which was the part where I kind of wondered if Sal and I should tiptoe away and pretend we'd never been there. I mean, obviously this was the best thing that had happened all week, but that still didn't mean I wanted to watch my grandparents making out on the promenade.

I coughed gently.

Gran and Grandad moved apart a tiny bit and looked across at us. They both had the same look in their eyes. I couldn't put my finger on it, but it was as if their eyes held the keys to a secret world, a world that no one else knew about. Then Grandad nodded toward us. "Let's sit," he said.

Sal and I shuffled along the bench as they came to join us.

Flake bounced between the two of them, shoving his head into Grandad's lap for a pat, then rubbing against Gran's legs.

Still holding Grandad's hand, Gran turned to me. "I always knew there was something odd going on," she said.

"With what?" I asked.

"All of it. Pip turning up out of nowhere, and never really explaining where he'd come from."

"Pip?" I said without thinking. It was so rare to hear Gran use Grandad's nickname that I wasn't sure who she was talking about for a moment.

"You know who I am, don't you?" Grandad said, looking at me intently. "You know who I *was*?"

I nodded. "I—I think so." For a moment, it felt too

ridiculous to say out loud. What if I was wrong? No, that was silly. I *knew* I wasn't wrong. "Peter?" I added in a squeak.

"I knew you'd have figured it out," Grandad said with a hint of a smile. "You remember our conversation on the beach when you told me your real name was Amelia but your friends called you Mia?" he went on. "When I found myself stranded in Luffsands, it hit me that I could do the same thing. So I made a fresh start with a new name. My middle name's Philip, so I decided to use that. Your gran's pet name for me was Pip."

I shook my head. My grandad — Pip — really *was* Peter. It was so much to take in.

Gran turned to me. "And then there was you, Mia, disappearing without trace," she went on. "There were so many unanswered questions back then."

"So how did you deal with them all?" I asked.

"I suppose there were too many other, more pressing, matters on my mind. After the storms and the move to the mainland, we all had to rebuild our lives, start again. I had Mother to look after. No time to sit and ponder a mystery that I would never get to the bottom of: the mysterious girl who came into my life only to disappear into thin air after helping to save my family's lives."

Suddenly, at least one thing made sense. The reason why Gran never talked about feelings; the reason she'd always believed in just getting on with things rather than lamenting and discussing everything. Because that's what she'd had to do as a child. She hadn't had time to sit around crying about it all; she'd had to hold her family together.

"Didn't you talk about it to anyone?" I asked.

Gran shook her head. "How could I? They still took girls my age into what we called lunatic asylums back then, you know. It would only have taken a signature from my father and I'd have been locked up for life."

I studied Gran's face. Was she joking? "What about Peter?" I asked. "I mean, Pip. Couldn't you talk to him?"

Gran smiled softly. "Ah, yes. So many times, it was on the tip of my tongue to ask. But you see, that was even more of a risk. To utter such questions to him and risk him thinking I was a crazy girl? No, I couldn't do it. Not when I knew I was falling in love with him. Too much had gone already. I had no home, no Luffsands, no island."

"You lost it all," I said quietly.

"Almost all. I still had friends — in fact, I could see more of them now. But it wasn't the same. They had no idea what I'd been through. Pip did. It was a bond like nothing I'd ever known, and Pip and my family and the other islanders were the only ones who shared it."

At the word "family," I suddenly realized something. Sal had been silent since Grandad had arrived.

Maybe it hit him at the same moment, I don't know. But just then, he turned to her, his eyes like pools about to overflow, and said in a whisper so soft it was like a wave lapping gently onto sand, "I've missed you."

At that, Sal shook her head. Biting hard on her bottom lip, she turned away. Then she stood up. "I can't handle this," she said, and started off back to the pub.

"Sal, wait!" Grandad called.

Gran put a hand on his arm. "Give her a moment," she said. "It's going to take time."

"I'll go," I said.

Grandad was standing, too. "No," he said. "We'll all go. They're as much my family as you are, and I owe *all* of you an explanation."

He reached out to help Gran up.

"Are you sure about this?" she asked.

Grandad's face was as firm as concrete. "I've never been more sure of anything." As I got up from the bench, he put his other arm around me. "This story has been locked up inside me for too long," he said. "And now that it's finally safe to do so, I need to tell it — to all of you."

Sal had joined her parents, and now she sat squashed into the bench seat with them in the lounge. Her eyes were red, her face hard and closed like a locked door. Mom was there, too.

As soon as we walked through the door, Mom leaped out of her chair as if it were on fire. "Dad!" she screamed, and ran over to throw her arms around him. "Dad! You're safe, you're safe," she said, over and over. When she pulled away from him, she had tears streaming down her face.

So did Grandad. But he wasn't looking at her. He was looking at Sal's dad, who was staring back at him. His expression was very different from Grandad's, though. I'd describe it as the way someone might look if a ghost walked into the room and politely asked if they'd like some coffee.

Sal's mom turned to look at Grandad and instantly her face turned pale. "Bernard?" she said, her voice a cracked whisper.

Grandad took a step closer to them. "I'm not Bernard," he said. His voice broke even more than hers had.

"Who's Bernard?" I asked.

"My grandpa," Sal replied woodenly.

"My father," her dad said.

"He died fifteen years ago," her mom added. "And he was the spitting image of this man."

Gran had disappeared into the kitchen and was coming back out with a couple of teacups. She poured some tea from the pot that was already on the table, then she sat down next to Mom.

Grandad sat next to her. I squeezed in at the other end of the bench seat, next to Sal.

Sal's dad looked confused. "If you're not Bernard," he asked, "who are you?"

Grandad took a deep breath, then slowly let it out. He held Sal's dad's gaze so firmly it was as though a laser beam connected them. "Dad, it's me," he said. "It's Peter."

Chapter Seventeen

I held my breath. I think everyone else did, too. The world held its breath and nothing moved; not the air, not a blink, nothing. Time stood still. Maybe literally. By now, I would have believed anything could happen.

Sal's mom was first to break the silence. "Who are you?" she whispered.

Grandad cleared his throat. "It's me, Mom," he said.

"Don't call me that!" Sal's mom snapped. "You must be thirty years older than me. I can't be your mother!"

Grandad nodded slowly. "I know," he said. "It's a lot to take in."

Sal's dad snorted. "Really? You *think*?"

Gran put a hand on Grandad's arm. "You've had a whole lifetime, remember," she said softly.

Sal's mom stared at Gran. "Who *is* this man?" she asked, her voice as taught as a wire.

Grandad reached out for her hand. "Mom, please believe me. I —"

She pulled her hand away. "How dare you! Coming here making fools of us at a time like this. Who do you think you are?"

"I keep *telling* you who I am," Grandad said, a blotchy rash reddening his neck as his frustration grew. "Why won't you believe me?"

Sal's mom's face turned gray. She was staring at Peter. "Your neck," she said.

Grandad reached up to touch his neck. "What about it?"

"The rash," she said simply. "That's what happens to Peter when he gets agitated."

Grandad met her eyes. "I know. I *am* Peter," he said.

The room fell silent. Eventually, his mom spoke again. "But how?" she asked. "How is such a thing possible?"

"You really want to know?" Grandad asked.

"Yes," Sal's dad — *his* dad — replied firmly. "We *need* to know."

"Well, it started a few months ago," Grandad began. "The town council had made some brochures, trying to bring some tourism to Porthaven."

"Brochures?" Sal's mom asked. "The ones advertising the fishing vacation?"

Grandad nodded.

"Wait — Gran told us about those," I butted in. "She said you acted all weird when they came around. And then you said you wanted to go away for the weekend."

"I always suspected that weekend away wasn't really a spontaneous romantic gesture," Gran said.

"It was that as well," Grandad said.

"But that wasn't the main reason for it," Gran insisted. "I realize that now. It was because of the brochure. You wanted to take it to your parent's house, didn't you?"

"*You* brought us that brochure?" Sal's mom said. "But why?"

Grandad took a deep breath. He clasped his hands in front of him as he let his breath back out in a long, low whistle. "I . . ." he began. His face had reddened. As I looked at him struggle to get the words out, it hit me. I knew what he was trying to say.

"You had to give it to Peter, didn't you?" I blurted out. "You had to deliver it to your younger self!"

I don't think I'd ever seen so many open jaws all at the same time. I could almost see the cogs working in everyone's brains as they tried to process this information. It was impossible — but it was true. I knew that now.

"Mia's right," Grandad said. "As soon as I saw the brochure a few months ago, I knew what it was. I recognized it as though I had seen it only yesterday."

"Even though, for you, the last time you'd seen it was actually fifty years ago," I said.

"Exactly. And that was when I finally understood why I'd had that blinding headache all those years ago as a child — the one that had me bedridden for almost the entire weekend."

"Two different versions of you came face-to-face!" I said. I'd seen the *Back to the Future* films. I knew the consequences of things like that. But this wasn't a film — it was real life. My family's life!

"Exactly," Grandad said. "Young me and old me were right there at the same time. As soon as I made the connection by looking right at myself, the pain was unbearable — for both of us. That day, I realized one thing: I couldn't go through that again. I wasn't sure either of us could survive it."

"Either of you?" Mom asked. She hadn't spoken up

till now, but she was hooked on every word of Grandad's story, just like the rest of us.

"Either version of myself," Grandad mumbled. "It's weird. Having the same moment twice, fifty years apart and from two different angles. Blew my mind. I dropped off the brochure and scurried away. Got to the end of the road. And then, even though I knew what would happen, I couldn't stop myself. I couldn't resist taking one quick glance at the boy I'd once been."

"And you were struck with a bad headache," I said.

Grandad snorted. "*Bad* doesn't even begin to describe it. Never had anything like it — apart from that other time."

"And that was the end of our romantic weekend," Gran said. "You spent the rest of it lying on the bed in the dark, moaning about how terrible you felt."

"Sorry," Grandad said sheepishly. Gran smiled and squeezed his hand in reply.

"That was when I knew I had done what I needed to do," he went on. "My family would come here for their vacation. I'd done my bit to ensure that would happen. But I had to be gone. There was no way I could afford to take the risk of something like that headache happening again. It could ruin everything."

"Ruin everything?" Mom asked.

"I had to make sure that young Peter was in Porthaven this week." Grandad turned to me. "He had to be here to meet you." Then he turned back to Gran and took her hands in his. "And to go to Luffsands for you." Holding her eyes with his, he went on. "That was why I *had* to leave. I couldn't risk Peter seeing me and being incapacitated by another headache — or worse."

Gran stared down at the hands wrapped around her own. "All these years, you held this in," she said. "Why did you never tell me?"

"How could he have?" I answered for him. Hearing Grandad's story made me realize he was the one who'd lost more than anyone in this. A whole lifetime without his family, and a lifetime of keeping the truth from his wife. "You've already told us what they did to crazy people. How would your family have reacted if he'd told you that he'd come from the future to save you all?"

"Mia's right," Grandad said. "So many times, I wanted to say something, and I almost did. But every time, the same thought stopped me. What if you thought I was crazy, or lying, or just a plain fool? What if I lost you? How could I try to convince you of something I could barely believe myself? So I kept my secret locked away in my heart. Carried it everywhere for fifty years. Gave everyone a glib lie about being an orphan boy on his travels when they asked where I'd come from."

"I've got a question," I said.

Grandad turned to me.

"How come you went over to Luffsands in the boat? You promised you wouldn't, but you did anyway."

Grandad lowered his face. Looking at the table, he replied, "You think I didn't ask myself that a thousand times?" He shook his head. "I wanted to surprise you. I thought, what's best—doing what I'm told, or trusting my abilities and making a bunch of other people smile? Not that there were many smiles that day."

"Maybe not," I said. "But think what could have happened if you hadn't gone. If you hadn't taken the boat and gone back to the Luffsands of fifty years ago."

Gran shuddered. "I don't even *want* to think about that."

Grandad nodded. "You're right," he said. "And given the chance, I'd do it all again."

Sal's parents were still staring at Grandad. Neither of them had spoken for a while. Their faces had completely drained of color.

"Peter," Sal's mom said eventually. "Is it really you? All this—it's really true?"

Grandad turned to her and nodded.

She had a tear rolling down each cheek, making identical tracks down her face.

Sal's dad swallowed. "Honestly?" he said. "This isn't some kind of joke?"

"Do I look as if I'm joking?" Grandad asked somberly.

"Look at him," Sal's mom said. "It's obvious. He's the spitting image of your father. Oh, Peter!"

With that, she got up and crossed over to sit beside Grandad. Wrapping her arms around his neck, she held him close. Grandad closed his eyes and held her, too.

"Your whole life," she whispered. "We've missed your whole life."

Grandad held her away from him and smiled faintly. "No, you haven't," he said. "I kept everything. I saved it for you. I knew this day would come, and I've prepared for it for fifty years."

"Your junk room!" Gran burst out. "Of course! *That's* what it was for. All those thousands of things I tried to make you get rid of."

"And I refused to throw out a single one," Grandad said, without taking his eyes off his mother. *His mother.* It seemed so strange to say it when she was probably about thirty years younger than him. But it was true. She was his mom. And Sal's dad was *his* dad. Which meant Sal was his sister. Sal who was still sitting back in her seat, silent and frowning, arms folded.

Grandad got up and nudged me to swap seats with him. I went to sit by Gran, and Grandad sat down where I'd been. "I know this is weird for you," he said to Sal.

"Weird? Really? Your brother goes missing and turns up the next day as an old man? Why would that be weird?"

"You're angry," Grandad said. "I understand."

Sal swiped a fist across her cheek. "I want my brother back," she said into her chest.

Grandad put an arm around her shoulder. "You've got him, I promise. And you're never going to get rid of him again, OK?"

Sal kept her arms folded and wouldn't reply.

"Sal." Grandad lifted her chin. "Look at me."

Sal looked at Grandad through heavy lids.

"It's me. It's Peter. I know it's weird—I know it's impossible. I know you'll probably never get over it—"

"Don't flatter yourself," Sal mumbled.

Grandad laughed. "That's more like it," he said.

Sal's mouth hinted at the beginnings of a smile.

"We'll work at it," Grandad said. "Together, as a family. Please, Sal. I've waited for this reunion for too many years. Don't spoil it for me now."

Sal leaned her head against Grandad's shoulder and let him pull her closer. "But what if you leave again?" she asked in a tiny voice.

"I'll *never* leave again," he said firmly.

Sal sniffed. "Promise?"

"I promise."

"But how can you? You live miles from us now."

"Yes, but remember, like I said, I've had a lot of time to plan this." Grandad smiled at Gran. "You know we've been wanting to retire for over a year?"

"Haven't we just," Gran replied. "Can't get anyone to take on the pub, though, can . . ." Her voice trailed away.

Grandad smiled at his parents. "We want you to take over," he said.

"You do?" his mom asked.

I looked at Gran. "Pip, don't be ridiculous," she said. "They can't just up and leave their home and jobs and —"

"Yes, we can!" Sal's dad said, grinning broadly. "Why on earth not? We've spent the last year with job losses looming over us. How about I just take the severance money and we go for it? A fresh start." He looked at Grandad. "For all of us," he added.

"It's the perfect solution," Grandad said, glancing at Gran, then back at his parents. "We'll all live here together, but you take over. It's your pub."

"Can we?" Sal asked.

"I . . . We . . . We'll talk about it, OK?" her mom said. "It's all happening a bit fast, but we'll think about it. It's definitely a possibility. No promises, though. Not yet."

Grandad nodded. Then he stood up and held his hand out. "Come upstairs to my study, Mom," he said. "I've got about twenty trunks full of photos I want to show you."

She stood up and took his hand. His dad had his hand on Grandad's back. "Come on, son. And don't skip a single thing."

It was weird hearing him call Grandad "son." It was weird hearing Grandad call a woman half his age "Mom." It was *all* weird. And yet, as the three of them went upstairs together to share a lifetime of memories, I realized that it didn't matter how weird it was. What mattered was that everyone had found one another again.

Which was when I realized something I'd found, too.

"Hey, Sal," I said, suddenly feeling shy.

She looked at me. "What?"

"You realize what this means, don't you?"

"It means we're not crazy. We didn't imagine it all."

I laughed. "Yeah, that as well. But even better than that . . . It means we're related." I stopped and scratched my head. "Kind of. I think."

She thought for a moment. Then her face broke out into the biggest smile I'd seen since I'd met her. It made her eyes sparkle and her cheeks glow. "Hey, I think you're right," she said. "We've both sort of got a new sister!"

"We sort of have!" I said, linking arms with her as we got up and went to join our families upstairs. "And, more importantly, we've both got a new *friend*."

"There's one thing I still don't understand," I said.

"What's that?" Grandad asked. We were walking along the beach, Flake running up ahead with Mitch, Mom in front of us with Sal's parents, and the rest of us in a line, buttoned up against the wind. We huddled a little closer together as we talked.

"The time-travel thing itself. How did it happen?"

Grandad laughed softly. "I asked myself that question a million times. I used to think your gran's father had it figured out. Those early days, something had rattled him good and proper — beyond the storm and what happened to the village. There was more to it than that. I could see it in his eyes, but he never spoke of it. And he never went back out in the boat, either. After we got to Porthaven, he didn't put a foot beyond the water's edge again."

"I never asked him why," Gran said. "I assumed the storm had taken his confidence away. It took so much else: our home, Mother's health. But we never had a conversation about it. Not once."

"We couldn't," Grandad said. "If we did, we knew it would open up so many other questions, and they were all either too painful or too confusing. It was as if we had a silent agreement that we would never speak of it."

"And we never did," said Gran, "until today."

"What happened to the boat?" Sal asked.

"Father sold it when we moved to the mainland," Gran said.

"First thing he did," Grandad added. "But to answer your question about the time travel, Mia . . . it wasn't till a few months later that I had an inkling." Grandad picked up a stick and threw it for the dogs. They raced each other across the sand, yapping and jumping around.

"About how the time travel actually happened, you mean?" I asked.

Grandad nodded. "When I first landed at Luffsands," he began, "it was all so dramatic. A massive wave had thrown me out of the boat. Thrown all sorts of other stuff out, too. I went underwater for what seemed like ages, and when I came up again, it had disappeared."

"The boat?"

"Yes. I thought it had sunk under a wave. I didn't think anything more about it until two things happened."

"What two things?" Sal asked.

"The first thing was when you two turned up. The boat obviously hadn't sunk at all, because you girls were on it! Which meant something else had made it disappear."

"It had traveled through time!" I said.

Grandad nodded. "Not that I registered the thought at the time. I was too busy holding on to a chimney for dear life."

"What was the second thing that happened?" Sal asked.

"It was when we went back to salvage what we could from all the wreckage. It was there, washed up on the beach."

"*What* was there?" I demanded.

Grandad looked at me. "The compass. I thought it must have gotten washed overboard at the same time I did."

That made sense. I remembered seeing how the stand looked as if it had come loose. "So the boat drifted back across to the mainland, but the compass washed up on Luffsands," I said.

"Exactly," Grandad agreed.

"You should have seen my father's face when we turned up with it," Gran said. "I'll never forget it."

"He wouldn't let the thing out of his sight, would he?" Grandad added. "The weird thing was, he'd sold the boat as soon as possible, but he held on to the compass for another couple of years. He used to sit looking at it, just staring at it, and scribbling stuff on a piece of paper. Never told us what he was writing, though."

"Or what he was thinking," Gran put in.

"Then one day, he went out and came back without it. Said he'd taken it back to where it had come from and he was glad to be rid of it."

"Did he say where that was?" I asked.

"Nope. And I never asked. But a couple of years after that, I was looking for some paperwork for something or other, and I came across the scrap of paper in a drawer. Full of scribbles and arrows and a big fat 'N' in the corner."

"That was the piece of paper we saw!" Sal blurted out.

"Exactly," Grandad said. "I couldn't help wondering why he'd held on to it, even though he'd gotten rid of the compass. I wanted to know what it was all about. I ended up sitting and looking at it for hours — a bit like he'd done — trying to find the clues among the scribbles."

"And did you find any?" I asked.

Grandad shook his head. "Not really. But I knew one thing. It had to have been important or he'd never have held on to it, so I put it back in the drawer. Then later that same week, I was out walking with your gran and I saw something that made me stop in my tracks. We were on the edge of town and we went past the boat shop."

"Shipshape," I said.

Grandad nodded. "And I don't know if it was because the paper with the scribbles was still fresh in my mind or what, but something suddenly clicked. A memory. I remembered you calling to me in the middle of the storm, remembered the name, Shipshape, and it hit me. *That* was where the compass had come from — and where it had been taken back to. I still didn't understand what had happened, but I knew then that I had one more thing to do in order to make sure things all worked out right."

"You had to make sure the compass got back to me," I said.

"Correct. Thankfully, it hadn't been sold."

Gran laughed. "Don't think I've ever seen much get sold at that place in all the years I've been here!"

"Luckily for us. So I went in and bought it — but I told him I wanted him to keep it. Then I put it in a bag and addressed it to you."

"And told the shopkeeper to give it to me!"

"Exactly. I put Pa's page of doodles with it. I still hadn't managed to make sense of them but I figured they were important somehow, and perhaps they'd mean something to you by the time you got them."

"And you scribbled a note on the back, so we knew we had to keep the compass with the boat," I added.

"That's right. Once I'd done all that, I could more or less forget about it — apart from the bit of my brain that never stopped trying to figure out exactly what *had* happened back then, and exactly what that 'N' was all about. I was pretty sure I'd been headed north when the shift in time happened. I reckoned the compass had hit north the moment that violent wave chucked me over the side. I was thrown off the boat, and the boat was somehow thrown forward in time in the same split second. So I was left behind —"

"Fifty years back in time," I said.

Grandad nodded. "But the boat came back to the present day and got washed up on the mainland."

"Which was how it ended up in that bay, waiting for us," I said.

We walked a few steps, watching the dogs run around in circles while we each processed all the new pieces of the puzzle. They were finally falling into place.

"The compass did that thing with us too," Sal said.

"I suspected as much," Grandad replied. "Tell me more."

"We were sailing north, and a gust of wind hit us from behind," I explained. "That was when it all went haywire. The compass needle started spinning and we ended up in the middle of nowhere."

"That was it, then," Grandad said. "That was how it happened."

"When the arrow pointed north and the wind hit from the south — it sent the compass spinning," I said.

"And somehow sent the boat back in time," Sal added.

"Whether there was anyone on it or not," I finished. "Which explains how Dee's dad could go to work on the mainland in his own time, but the boat could slip into *our* time. It must have happened when it moved around on its mooring so that it was facing north and then a gust of wind hit it from the south."

"Apart from the time it must have happened while he was still on it," Sal said. "The time when he somehow ended up on the mainland in *our* time, not his."

"And then again when we sent him back home," I added.

Grandad let out a whistle. "That's pretty much it in a nutshell, then."

"So it never happened again?" I asked.

Grandad shook his head. "Never had the chance. Chap who bought the boat wasn't from around here, so the boat and compass were separated straightaway. But before I took the note to the shop and packaged up the compass for you, I made a decision that it was time to leave the past behind and look to the future." He winked at Gran. "And I had a plan for that as well."

"What was that?" I asked.

Grandad threw an arm around Gran's shoulders. "I had to marry the girl I'd loved since I'd first set eyes on her."

Gran rested her head on Grandad's shoulder and slung an arm around his waist. The smile they gave each other said more than any words could have.

"Hey, Grandad," I said as we walked on. "I've just had another thought."

"What's that?"

"The permission letter at the lifeboat station. How come you'd already written one for me?"

Grandad smiled. "Remember, I still didn't know exactly how you had managed to get back to us all those years ago, and I had never been able to talk about it with anyone. I recalled you saying that you were going to fetch the lifeboat men, and even though I never saw you again after that, I remembered your words when the piece about the lifeboat open house turned up in last week's *Times & Echo*."

"So you thought you'd make sure you'd covered all the bases," I concluded.

"Exactly. I figured it couldn't do any harm."

At that moment, Flake came running over and dropped a stick at Grandad's feet, pulling our attention back to the present day. Mitch stood a little farther away, furiously wagging his tiny tail too, his little pink tongue sticking out as he panted.

Grandad looked down at the stick, and then at Flake. "Want me to throw this, do you?" he asked.

In reply, Flake wagged his tail so furiously it swept an arc in the sand.

Grandad laughed and threw the stick. Flake ran and grabbed it instantly. I bent down and threw another one for Mitch, and before long the two of them were chasing each other around in circles again.

We walked along in silence for a few moments, catching up with Mom and Sal's parents. I looked across the water. The sun was trying to come out and there were tiny patches of light sparkling on the surface of the sea.

"I wonder what happened to the boat," I said.

"Maybe it broke up on some rocks," suggested Sal.

"Or got sold to a pirate," her mom said, linking her arm with Sal's.

"Might have gotten chopped up for firewood," said her dad.

"Or raised onto stilts and put in someone's back-yard," Mom added.

"Could be anywhere," Grandad replied. "It's for someone else's journey now, though. I think we've reached our destination."

As the others walked along the beach, smiling and laughing, I paused to look out to sea. There was a piece of driftwood bobbing around on the waves near the beach. The sunlight caught the edge of it and, for a moment, seemed to make it glow yellow like the hull of the boat.

I stared at the driftwood, wondering if maybe it *was* a piece of the boat; if perhaps it was still here, all around us; if the boat and compass had been sent just for us or if they traveled constantly through time, bringing people together, mending links and building bridges across the chasms that split people's lives apart.

A moment later, the sunlight moved away, and the driftwood washed up onto the shore. It was beckoning me, teasing me, inviting me back to the water's edge.

But I didn't want to go back.

I watched it a moment longer. And then I turned away and ran along the beach to join my family.

Eric

It had been a quiet day at the boat shop. So quiet, in fact, that Eric was considering closing early. He rolled himself a cigarette and riffled through some papers in the back office. He'd close up in ten minutes.

He had just put his cigarette out when a man burst through the door. He scoured the shop, looking down every aisle till he found the one with the compasses.

"Looking for anything in particular?" Eric asked.

The man didn't reply. He was so intent on his close inspection of the compasses that he probably hadn't even heard Eric speak.

"That's it!" the man suddenly said, a few moments later. He picked up one of the compasses and carried it to the desk.

"That one, is it?" Eric asked, grabbing a plastic bag to put it in.

The man nodded. "But I don't want to take it away," he said. "I want you to keep it." Then he pulled a wad of cash and a piece of paper from his pocket and held them both out toward Eric. "Can you take this note?" he asked. "Put it in the bag with the compass."

Eric studied the man. Quite sharp looking. Mid-twenties. Bright shiny new band on his wedding finger.

"Put it with the compass and keep them both here?" Eric asked the man. "Why would I do that?"

"I — it's for someone. I need to leave it here for them."

"You're not mistaking me for a post office, are you?" Eric asked, narrowing his eyes.

"No. I — I just need to leave it here. Please. It's for a friend."

Eric studied the man a moment longer. "For a friend," he repeated. Then he took the paper from him.

"Yes," the man said.

"And what does this friend look like?" Eric asked, slipping the paper inside the bag.

"She . . . well, she's a girl. Thirteen years old. Normal

sort of height for a girl her age. Quite skinny. Blond hair—about shoulder length, maybe a bit longer." The man watched as Eric put the compass inside the bag. Then, casting his eyes across the desk in between them, he pointed at a marker. "Can I borrow your pen?"

Eric shrugged and passed the pen across.

The man picked up the bag from the desk and pulled out the piece of paper. He wrote something quickly and put it back in the bag. Then he scribbled something on the side of the package, before holding it out to Eric.

Eric squinted at the bag. "For Mia?" he said, raising an eyebrow.

"That's her name."

"I see. And this Mia—will she be expecting a package?"

"I'm not sure. I don't think so."

"So what makes you think she'll be coming in, then?"

The young man looked Eric in the eye. "She'll be here," he said firmly. "She'll have a poster with her. She'll be looking for someone. For . . . well, for someone who looks like a slightly younger version of me. Please, just pass it on. Tell her it's from Pi—from Peter."

"Peter."

The young man nodded. Eric held his gaze for so long that Peter began to fidget. Clasping his hands

263

together, he twisted the shiny ring around and around on his finger.

Eric pointed at the ring. "New?"

Peter smiled. "Just married."

Eric nodded slowly. Finally, he spoke again. "OK, then. I'll do it for you."

"Thank you," Peter said. "Thank you!" His face was a wide smile of relief as he turned to leave. But halfway back to the door, he stopped.

Turning back to Eric, he cleared his throat. A hint of red edged across his neck. "There's one more thing," he said.

Eric waited.

Peter paused, his eyes darting around as if he were searching the shop for the words he needed. "You may have to hold on to it for a while," he said eventually. Then his eyes met Eric's and held them firmly. "But she will come for it," he added. "I promise. One day, she'll be here."

ACKNOWLEDGMENTS

With enormous thanks to the many people who helped me to turn a moment of inspiration into an actual book.

As always, my family was extremely helpful and supportive in all their varied and wonderful ways. Thank you for being amongst the first and last to check each book for me.

Huge gratitude, as always, to my kindest critic, biggest fan, and best friend, Laura Tonge.

Thanks also to my top writer buddy Annabel Pitcher, for our ingenious scheme to support each other in our writing and reward each other with books!

I am possibly more grateful with every book to my wonderful publishers Orion and Candlewick. Thank you for continuing to have faith in me and my books, and for all the many, many things you do for them and for me.

Eternal gratitude to my agent Catherine Clarke — the best in the business!

And finally, a massive thank you to the lovely Pink Bag Lady, Jane Cooper, who came up with the perfect title after I had spent about a year discarding hundreds of others and driving all my friends mad in the search for the right one.

Dive in and read the
New York Times *best-selling series!*

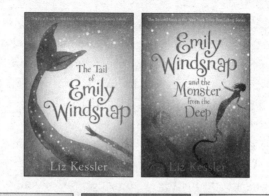